He felt more at peace than he had since the accident happened.

In that moment, he didn't feel like a patient. He felt like Noah Breedlove, and he uttered his gratitude to Damaris.

"What did you say?"

"I said..." His eyes fluttered open to find Damaris's head bent low to hear his whisper, those luscious lips mere inches from his own. He raised his hand, placed it behind her neck and pulled her face closer.

"Thank you."

Her lips were even softer than he imagined, her touch, tentative. He expected her to pull back. Instead, she increased the pressure. That simple act of acquiescence was like a starter gun at the Kentucky derby, his passion like a Thoroughbred shooting out of the gate.

His hand slid into her thick tresses at the same time his tongue pressed through her slightly parted lips. Their tongues met and danced—slowly swirling, tasting.

"Noah..."

* * *

Sin City Seduction by Zuri Day is part of the Sin City Secrets series.

Dear Reader,

When preparing to write you this letter, the last thing I expected was to become all deep and philosophical. *It's a romance novel, chick. Lighten up!* But that's what happened, and I realize why.

Noah's story opened me up to an "other," took me into a world I'd not travelled before—the world of people with disabilities. Did you know that almost fifty million Americans live with some form of disability, and almost a billion people worldwide? Before researching Noah's story, I didn't. Hadn't given the subject much thought. In doing the research and getting to know him, however, I became more aware of a journey through life that looked different than mine and came away more enlightened about and empathetic to how those with disabilities navigate a world without some of the things that I take for granted. Like standing. Walking. Using the restroom unaided.

I was reminded that what makes us powerful is not the ability to dismiss a part of another person in order to accept them, such as those well-meaning individuals who say, "I don't see color," for instance. But rather to look with eyes wide open at all that makes us different yet focus on and appreciate the many ways we are the same. Like all of us romance lovers who love a good happily-ever-after.

I see you, DayDreamers, in all of your uniqueness. What a beautiful bouquet!

Zuri Day

ZURI DAY

SIN CITY SEDUCTION

HARLEQUIN®
DESIRE™

PLEASE RECYCLE
THIS PRODUCT IS RECYCLABLE

Recycling programs
for this product may
not exist in your area.

ISBN-13: 978-1-335-20928-3

Sin City Seduction

Harlequin Enterprises ULC
22 Adelaide St. West, 40th Floor
Toronto, Ontario M5H 4E3, Canada
www.Harlequin.com

Zuri Day is the nationally bestselling author of two dozen novels, including the popular Drakes of California series. She is a winner of the RSJ Emma Award, the AALAS (African American Literary Awards Show) Best Romance Award and others, and a finalist for multiple RT Reviewers' Choice Best Book Awards in Multicultural Fiction. Find out more and stay in touch at zuriday.com.

Books by Zuri Day

Harlequin Desire

Sin City Secrets

Sin City Vows
Ready for the Rancher
Sin City Seduction

Harlequin Kimani Romance

Champagne Kisses
Platinum Promises
Solid Gold Seduction
Secret Silver Nights
Crystal Caress

Visit her Author Profile page at Harlequin.com, or zuriday.com, for more titles.

You can also find Zuri Day on Facebook, along with other Harlequin Desire authors, at Facebook.com/harlequindesireauthors!

Life is an adventure,
often full of surprises,

Between the star-filled nights
and inspiring sunrises.

Ironic that those experiences
that are our hardest tests,

Are often the ones that lead us into
being our absolute best.

One

Clear skies. Light breeze. Bright sun. Firm snow. Noah Breedlove stood near the summit of the mountain and felt he was on top of the world. He was one opponent and a council vote away from closing his first solo business deal in a city that detractors had deemed off-limits to CANN International. Had they missed the meaning behind the company name, to have the skill, power or ability to do anything? That Breedloves could and did, every single day? Just as he'd vanquished almost every obstacle in the boardroom, all save that one lonely hold-out, he now stood ready to conquer this legendary mountain in Manning Valley, two hours away from Salt Lake City. Hopefully the adventuresome trip down the mountain would clear his head and help ease the stress he felt at trying to close the biggest deal he'd ever done.

"You ready?"

Noah looked at Cole, the friend who'd introduced him to skiing, with a trademark Breedlove smile—twinkling eyes, winking dimple, sparkling teeth.

"Born that way."

"I know you're a pro, bro, but be careful," Cole said. "The speed of this mountain has felled lesser men."

Noah surveyed the terrain marked on maps by a double black diamond, a designation given to a resort's toughest runs. Narrow slopes, wicked turns and a virtual obstacle course of tall pines and craggy rocks loomed before him. Noah wasn't worried. He might look like a daredevil but really he wasn't. It was confidence in skill level and preparation that fueled his desire. Okay, maybe a tiny part of it was due to the thrill. If life weren't dangerous, it wouldn't be fun.

They pushed off, straight down the chute. Noah tucked his poles and flew like the wind. He slid around trees and jumped over rocks, his lithe, toned body soaring before landing with ease. Life was perfect! Couldn't be better!

They didn't see the thin white rope until right up on it. Cole managed to ski around it. Noah jumped it but his ski caught, causing a forty-foot tumble. His world went black.

Damaris Glen looked up as a bustle of activity interrupted an otherwise quiet evening. She was already halfway out of her chair when her assistant nurse and newfound friend, Wendy, stuck her head through the office door.

"What do we have?" Damaris asked, quickly checking for her stethoscope and stuffing a notepad and pen in her pocket as they sped toward the emergency department's lobby.

"Skiing accident. EMT's en route."

"How serious?"

"The patient's unconscious." Wendy's voice was casual, but her cornflower blue eyes conveyed a concern that was anything but.

"Dr. Noble?"

"Left an hour ago," Wendy continued at Damaris's questioning glance. She shrugged. "Slow night. He's on his way back now."

Damaris's heartbeat quickened. This was the first week not shadowing Ella, her supervisor. Her first night in charge of the team. Though she'd been extensively trained in how to receive and perform the intake and treatment on trauma patients, it was something nurses did only when a doctor wasn't present. Or on call. Like tonight. "Rarely happens," was Ella's answer when Damaris had presented this very scenario. Meanwhile "rarely" lay on a stretcher with an EMT beside him.

A calm settled around her shoulders as Damaris approached. She made eye contact with the EMT and gave a quick nod, but her first words were to the man lying prone on the gurney.

"Hello, are you awake? Can you hear me?" She placed a palm on his forehead, her other thumb on a wrist, taking his pulse. She was every inch the professional, but still, it registered that beneath the cuts and bruises was a very handsome man. Barely noted. Not acknowledged. Doing such was hardly a part of her job.

She looked at the EMT. "Has he spoken at all?"

The woman shook her head. "All of what we obtained came from the friend skiing with him. It's all here." She held out the report containing information gathered en route.

Damaris scanned the paper. "Vitals?"

"Stabilized," the EMT said.

"Do we know how the accident happened?"

"The friend who called 911 said a line of some kind was obstructing the trail, too thin to see until they were right up on it. He was far enough behind our guy here to clear the obstruction, once he knew it was there."

"Where is this friend?"

An obviously distraught man came around the corner and rushed toward them. "Is he awake? Noah!" He stepped toward the stretcher.

Damaris placed a hand on his shoulder as she spoke to the EMT. "We'll take it from here. Thanks."

She turned back to the harried-looking man still wearing skiwear and boots. "Are you the friend who called for help?"

He nodded.

"What's your name?"

"Cole." His voice crackled with emotion as he looked over her shoulder. "Is he going to be okay?"

"He's stabilized and we're doing all we can. The doctor is on his way. I know this is hard but, please, try to calm down. We'll need you to tell the doctor everything you can remember," she continued, her voice low and soothing.

Cole nodded. "His name is Noah. Everything happened so fast! I called his family and they're on their way but we live in Nevada so it's going to take a while for them to get here. I'm the one who got him into skiing and if anything happens…"

Working as a trauma nurse was understandably difficult and dealing with the patients' loved ones was one of the hardest parts.

"We're going to do everything we can to help... Noah...right?"

"Yeah."

Damaris watched the distraught man gain control of his emotions, almost angrily swiping tears from his face. She gave his arm a comforting squeeze.

The sliding glass doors opened. A blast of cold air lifted the curls from Damaris's face. "Dr. Noble."

A thin man with wire-rimmed glasses and a friendly face walked over, his eyes on the stretcher. "Any change?"

Damaris quickly updated the doctor. The friend, Cole, now calmer, filled in the blanks not known by the EMT.

Dr. Noble turned to Damaris. "We need a CAT scan and a complete set of X-rays stat."

"Right away, Doctor."

The doctor left to check on other patients. Within minutes a technician arrived. Damaris directed the move to another room, where the patient was transferred to a trauma X-ray stretcher so that his spine could be viewed and analyzed while lying down. Damaris stayed beside the man she now knew as Noah, explaining procedures and offering encouragement even though he'd not moved. The technicians finished their work. Cole left to contact the family and give them an update. Damaris stayed, monitored his vitals and kept talking.

"Some believe that when our body shuts down and our mind closes out the rest of the world, it is so the body can protect itself, take an assessment of the situation and begin healing."

She watched his face for a twitch, a flutter, any movement to indicate he may have heard her. Nothing. Again, she was struck by the sharp, arresting features discernible beneath the bruising and scars. As she took a cursory examination of these facial wounds, she felt a stirring in her heart for this stranger that seeped into her soul, a stake so immediately and deeply invested in his recovery that it scared her. *I'm a caring, compassionate nurse, passionate about healing.* Healing, not heartthrobs, she told herself. Of course she'd care. It was her empathetic nature and when it came to the welfare of her patients she'd always felt this way. Hadn't she? Not really, but she forced herself to ignore this fact. There was no point in developing feelings for someone outside her faith. She'd done that once before and it had cost her. Big-time. She was still weighed down by the guilt.

"Noah, your friend Cole has contacted your parents. I'm sure they're on their way. My name is Damaris but that's a mouthful so most people call me Dee. I'm the lead nurse this shift and am here to keep an eye on you until the doctor returns and your family arrives. I hope you won't mind that I say a little prayer that by the time they get here, you will have regained consciousness."

Like many citizens of the Beehive State, religion was a central part of Damaris's family and very important to her. She believed in Western medicine and its power to heal, but felt it didn't hurt to add a little faith. Closing her eyes, she whispered a quick prayer. A strong sensation caused her to open them before she'd said amen. Staring back at her was the most beautiful pair of eyes she'd ever seen.

"You're awake."

She watched him swallow, attempting to talk.

"Do you remember what happened?"

He shook his head.

"You were skiing with your friend Cole and took a bad fall," she said, answering the question in his eyes as she reached his bedside and rang the nurses' station. "Your mouth is probably dry and you may be thirsty but I'm afraid I can't offer you water right now."

The intercom dinged. "Yes?"

"Wendy, can you tell the doctor that our patient is awake?"

"Sure."

Damaris returned her attention to Noah. "The doctor will be here shortly."

She noted that along with the large cuts on his forehead and chin, his lips were dry and cracked. "You've got a couple nasty cuts," she continued, crossing over to a set of drawers and retrieving several items. "I'll clean them out and apply medication that I hope will make them feel a little better."

He watched her every move. She knew it. Not because she possessed eyes in the back of her head, as her mom did, but because the intensity in those dark brown orbs felt like lasers at her back. No doubt he was in pain, probably confused, too. Still, he hadn't asked a question. Hadn't made a sound. Shock? Calm personality? Who knew? She'd be distraught.

After gathering cotton swabs, astringent and other medications, and a towel, Damaris filled a small paper cup with water and placed everything on a steel tray that she wheeled next to the bed. She dabbed a corner of the towel into the water.

"This will help the dryness a bit."

She reached toward his mouth. His hand shot up. The move was quick, unexpected. His eyes, searching, lips, moving, trying to talk.

"Is there pain?" Damaris asked.

He shook his head.

"Thirsty? Anxious?"

No on both counts.

She watched as he flicked his tongue against the lips she would have dampened, cleared his throat and uttered his first words since entering the hospital.

"I can't move my legs."

Damaris heard a mix of fear, panic and disbelief wrapped around those five words. She tried to address all three, simultaneously. "It's okay. Try to—"

"Nothing's okay. Didn't you hear me?" he continued, hoarseness coating the words he forced out with effort. "My legs. I can't move them."

"I'm sorry. What I meant was—"

"I hear we have an awakened patient," Dr. Noble said as he entered the room. "I'm Dr. Noble. You took quite a fall, young man. We're going to do our best to get you back up and running, okay?"

Damaris was grateful for backup. She moved the tray away from the bed so that the doctor could move freely around the X-ray stretcher, then hurried back to his side, ready to assist.

"My legs, Doctor. I've been trying to lift them, change positions, but nothing seems to work. I can't really feel them, either."

"There can be many reasons for that." Much as was Damaris's manner, Dr. Noble calmly chatted as he worked, examining the image on the X-ray screen before folding back the sheet from Noah's lower legs. "As I stated, you took a mean tumble. Your body is probably in shock, a state where the mind's call and the body's response have a hard time singing together, if you know what I mean."

A lover of music no matter the genre, Damaris understood the doctor's metaphor. She smiled encouragingly at Noah, who'd shifted those laser beams he had for eyes in her direction. His expression remained serious, almost haunting. Somehow she understood that, too.

She checked her watch. "Doctor, should I have another nurse make my rounds?"

"I think we're good here," he replied with a nod. "I'm going to perform a few tests and then we'll get you down for a CAT scan. All right?"

Noah nodded.

"You're in good hands," she told Noah, walking toward the door.

"You sure are," Dr. Noble agreed. "Dee is one of the best nurses in the building."

She smirked at the doctor, gave her silent, observant patient a wave and headed back to the wing she was in charge of. Checking in with the other patients, Damaris was efficient and friendly, giving them her undivided attention as best she could. But much as Noah seemed to be experiencing, and as the doctor described, her call and response weren't keeping the same tune. Her body went from room to room performing as needed. A part of her mind, however, remained back in the room with the accident victim who possessed a steely demeanor in the face of crisis, and a pair of intensely beautiful eyes.

Two

Images played across his mind like a movie reel. Snatches of moments from earlier that day. The flight into Salt Lake City. Meeting with council members and others to discuss his ambitious plans for opening the first legal casino in a no-gambling state. Climbing into Cole's rental car for the two-hour drive to Daredevil Mountain, sometimes called Death Mountain because fatal accidents had occurred on the extreme slope. Casual chitchat and laughter as they laced on their skis. Boarding a lift and zooming straight to the top. The whoosh of the wind as he pushed off from the ledge. Then…waking up and feeling disconcerted, an angel with curly hair and bright eyes hovering over his bed. What was her name? Delores? Naturally beautiful, at least in his mind. So much so she appeared otherworldly, made him consider the notion that heaven was real. He shifted, or tried to, and remembered something else, something he'd rather not think about. He couldn't move his legs. Which meant he couldn't walk. Could the angel he remembered perform miracles and make his legs work again?

A commotion in the hallway caught Noah's attention. Familiar voices drifted down the hall. Seconds later, the private suite where he'd been transferred to opened. His mom, Victoria, rushed into the room. Just behind her was his dad, Nicholas, one of his brothers, Adam, and Adam's wife, Ryan. The love and concern in all of their eyes felt like a warm blanket that covered him whole. His legs weren't responding but his heart felt plenty. He accepted his mother's hug and fought to control his emotions.

"Oh, baby. Look at you!" Victoria touched, then kissed the bandages that covered his facial injuries as though he were a child. "I'm so sorry you've been here this long without us. We got here just as quickly as we could."

"Mom! I can't move my legs."

"I know, son. The doctor said…" Victoria stepped back.

Her words had stopped with a quick shake of Nicholas's head. "Son."

Noah looked from one parent to the other. "What?"

Nicholas didn't answer. Noah's sister-in-law, Ryan, stepped forward. A naturopathic practitioner with a growing practice in Las Vegas, her bedside manner was gentle and comforting, with an air of authority that eased Noah's anxiety.

"Hey there, brother-in-love. The doctor spoke to us briefly just before we came into your room. He's not sure what's going on with you physically just yet. They're waiting for the results of the CAT scan. Until we know exactly what's going on, it's better not to speculate and for you to remain as still, calm and positive as possible."

Noah wasn't placated. "I know you mean well, Ryan, but that's hard to do. What does he think is going on? Does he think this situation with my legs might be permanent, that I'll never walk again?"

"Again, he doesn't want to speculate and neither should you. If something is strained, fractured or broken, keeping movement to a minimum will keep further damage from being done."

"Wait!" Noah's face brightened. "My body could just be in shock, right? The doctor said something like that earlier. My brain still feels jumbled from the fall, but I think that's what he told me."

"That's very possible," Ryan said. "Shock is one way the body protects itself."

The body protecting itself. He'd heard that earlier, too. Was it the doctor who'd said it? Noah's brow furrowed with the effort to untangle the thoughts in his brain.

"Son, are you feeling pain?"

Noah looked at his everyday-alpha father and was moved by the tenderness with which Nicholas spoke. "Only like I got beat up in a barroom brawl, then run over by a train."

Adam stepped forward. "But other than that, you're okay?"

Everyone laughed. The atmosphere lightened.

Victoria perched herself on a side of the bed and ran a hand over Noah's soft curls. "Your grandparents know about what happened and send their love. They wanted to be here but with Papa still battling a bout of bronchitis, Mama Jewel didn't want to chance him leaving the home."

"Where's Twin?"

"Christian and Nick are still in Africa, honey. Tomorrow morning, they'll take the first flight out."

As much as Noah wanted to see his twin, Nick, right now, the resort in Djibouti was his oldest brother Christian's baby. The first phase of the latest hotel construction was nearing completion. Christian should stay there and since Nick would be selling the pricey units, he needed to be there, too.

"Is that really necessary? My immobility is probably just due to shock. By the time they fly here from Africa, I may be released and beat them home."

"In that case they'll arrive in time for a celebratory dinner," Victoria said. "Once they learned about your accident, nothing else mattered."

"Yeah, man, I had to calm down your double," Adam explained. "Had he not been able to find a seat on an airline, Nick would have donned a cape and flown on his own."

The group kept up a lively chatter, until the door opened. A nurse entered that Noah didn't remember seeing before. His eyes remained on the door, subconsciously hoping someone else would walk in behind him. Her, the angel from yesterday. His heart dropped a notch when she didn't appear. The nurse checked his vitals and recommended he get much-needed rest. Within minutes of his family leaving, Noah fell asleep.

When he woke up, the angel had returned. Unfortunately, the happy mood generated by his family the day before had evaporated, replaced by a swirling of negative emotions over the very real possibility that he may never walk again.

"Good morning, Noah!"

"What's good about it?"

He noted the slightest of reactions, the merest widening of those gorgeous brown eyes, before Damaris responded, accompanied by another of her sunshine smiles. "My grandmother would say that any day waking up outside the coffin is a pretty good one."

"Was your grandmother paralyzed?"

Her smile fled faster than sprinter Usain Bolt leaped from starter blocks. "No." She took a breath. He could almost see a professional mask slip into place as she viewed the machines and began recording his vitals. Noah felt bad for snapping at her. She was only trying to make him feel better, seemed to be diligent in attending to him now and had nothing to do with why he was here. How the accident happened was something he was still trying to figure out.

"I'm sorry."

"I forgive you," she responded, almost before the apology was fully out. The warmth immediately returned to her voice.

"I've not been in your shoes and can't judge your reaction. To say it must be extremely hard is probably an understatement. But what we think about we tend to bring about so maybe thinking positive would be in your best interest right now."

"What we think about we bring about. Another quote from Grandma?"

Damaris shook her head. "I heard that one in college, not sure who coined the phrase. Most of Grandma's quotes were from the bible. She believed in the scriptures and the power of prayer."

"Yeah, well, I'm not into scriptures and am not a praying man."

Their conversation was interrupted when the Breed-loves arrived seven persons strong. Noah's skiing friend, Cole, was with them, too. Nicholas, Victoria, Adam and his wife, Ryan, who came yesterday, were joined by Noah's twin, Nick, brother Christian and Christian's wife, Lauren. They'd barely finished their hellos when Dr. Noble entered the room.

"I've got some good news and some that's a bit more challenging," Dr. Noble said after greeting the group and attaching several X-rays to a wall screen. "Which do you want first?"

"The bad news," Noah said.

"The good news," both Victoria and Ryan chimed at the same time.

Dr. Noble focused on Noah. "The challenging news," he continued, "is that the lack of movement in your legs is not due to shock. Had that been the case, you may have regained feeling and use already, at least in a limited capacity."

He pulled out a pointer. "Here's what's going on. These areas here are where major bruising occurred to your spinal cord, affecting the nerves controlling leg movement and other functions. The good news is that there are no fractures or breaks. With time, physical therapy and a positive attitude, you'll most likely regain full use of all your extremities."

There was that phrase again. Positive attitude. If heard for a third time Noah thought he might puke. "What kind of time are we talking?"

"Some take weeks, others months. It's hard to say."

"For now, though, I'm paralyzed?"

"You're suffering a temporary paralysis, yes."

For the second time in less than twenty-four hours,

Noah's world went dark. A mental blackout this time but the results was the same. He'd recall very little of what was said after hearing *paralysis* come from the doctor's mouth, or what his family said as they tried to cheer him. He'd barely said ten words to his best friend, Cole, who somehow blamed himself for the accident, and dismissed the use of *temporary* to describe the condition, felt it a description that only prolonged the inevitable truth. He couldn't walk. Not now, maybe not ever again. With every thought of how not walking affected his lifestyle, Noah's outlook worsened. By the time his "angel" of a nurse arrived on the scene, once again, he was in a devil kind of mood.

He braced himself for her cheery good-morning, fully prepared to tear into her, and without apology this time. But as she approached his bed, she wasn't smiling. She caught and held his gaze. The compassion and empathy that fairly beamed from her eyes was intense to the point of being unnerving.

"I don't want your pity," he mumbled, but not low enough.

"Good, because I have none to give you." She began her daily ministrations in checking his health. "It's the last thing you need, especially now, when there is a chance that you'll walk again. It will not be an easy road, but at least you have one. My pity is reserved for the person who is told, without a shadow of a doubt in the doctor's mind, that they will never walk, or stand on their own power, or if quadriplegic, never again experience total independence."

She came back around to face him, meeting his intense gaze with one of her own. "What happened to you, Noah, is very unfortunate. And while you probably don't want to hear it, you need to understand how blessed you are to have been brought down Death Mountain on a stretcher and not in a body bag."

Her face softened, while her demeanor remained professional and authoritative. "The doctor will be in shortly, along with a physical therapist. They're going to perform a series of tests to try to determine the extent of the paralysis and what, if any, exercises you can begin to do right away. It's important to keep as many of your muscles as active as possible. It may be a fairly intense exercise so until then, try to get some rest."

With the merest of smiles she turned and walked out of the room, leaving Noah to digest what he'd just witnessed, someone who'd told him in no uncertain terms exactly what she thought of him and his behavior. He would never have guessed that the warm, bubbly person who'd entered his room was capable of being the strong, commanding woman who'd left it. Obviously, there were many layers to the nurse whose name he couldn't recall. He found the thought of discovering just how many an intriguing notion. Not the only thing he wanted, but a start. He wanted to walk again, too, preferably out of the hospital. And he planned to make it clear that building a CANN Casino Hotel and Spa in Utah wasn't just in the best interest of CANN International. But for those who opposed it, too.

Three

While attending to her other patients, Noah stayed on Damaris's mind. His ongoing negative attitude was not only annoying but concerning, as well. Attitude played a huge role in how quickly a person healed, to what degree they improved and sometimes whether or not there was any change at all. In giving Noah the highest and best treatment she possibly could, she felt it was her responsibility to share what she knew with his family and encourage them to try to keep his spirits high. Dr. Noble had his hands full trying to heal Noah's body. Damaris would focus on his mind.

Her chance came the next afternoon. She arrived for her shift and learned that Noah would soon be moved to the rehabilitation unit. Dr. Noble called together the family to discuss the proposed treatment and physical therapy regimen for the remaining two weeks Noah would be at the hospital and how to prepare for his return home. Once done and with their questions answered, Dr. Noble hurried to his next patient. Damaris watched the family head in the opposite direction, the parking lot most likely. She'd see less of them once Noah was moved to the rehabilitation ward and didn't want to miss the chance of speaking one-on-one with Victoria. She set her tablet on the nurses' station counter and hurried after the group.

"Mrs. Breedlove?"

Victoria paused, and turned. So did everyone else. Unrelenting gazes from curious faces all trained on her.

"Yes?"

Damaris observed the sophisticated, close-knit family, the runway-ready women and *GQ*-looking men, and became intimidated. She watched Victoria break away from the group and walk toward her. The trepidation increased. Who was she, a rather sheltered girl growing up in a small community outside Salt Lake City, to give advice to a worldly, sophisticated woman like Victoria Breedlove, one who—if what she'd overheard earlier was correct—belonged to one of the richest families in the United States?

You're a well-qualified, well-trained, well-educated nurse who knows what she's doing, came the response from something inside her. Damaris took a breath, smiled warmly at Victoria as she did so and continued to approach.

"May I speak with you for a second?"

"Sure," Victoria answered. She turned to the others. "I'll catch up, guys."

"We'll wait in the lobby," her husband responded.

"This is probably something that Dr. Noble has already done and is not officially my place as a nurse. But I saw such concern on your face regarding Noah. I wanted to offer some encouragement regarding his situation, and if you're interested, a little advice."

"That's very sweet of you," Victoria looked down to read her name tag. "'Da…'"

"Damaris," she said. "Most of my friends call me Dee."

"Dee is easier, but Damaris is lovely, as is your desire to help me navigate this process. I can truly use any and all the assistance available. My family has never dealt with anything like this. Noah's life has been relatively problem-free. He's a good kid—smart, hard worker, focused. I can't remember a time when he hasn't been fully in control of his life. Even as a child. Which has me deeply worried about how he'll rise to this challenge, not only the physical aspect but his mental and emotional frame of mind."

Bolstered by Victoria's words and made comfortable by her laid-back demeanor, Damaris suggested they cross the hall to a small seating area. Once facing each other on a love seat positioned across from a coffee table and two chairs, she continued.

"Though probably unlike Noah, the reactions he's exhibited are fairly typical of those who find their lives flipped upside down. If the person is strong-willed, independent and used to being in control of their life and circumstances, as you've described your son, it's especially difficult. Even with a temporary loss of movement, there's a grieving process that involves some of everything we've seen—anger, sadness, denial, depression. I haven't been in the field very long but, from what I've seen so far, most do come to grips with their new reality and make the necessary adjustments to have a productive life."

"As I said, Noah is very focused and determined. He's conquered everything that he's tried."

"Those traits will go a long way toward his healing. Another very important component is his overall attitude. Again, it's understandable that he's upset about life's prospects right now. It's important that the family be as upbeat and positive as possible, to not let him wallow in negativity or self-pity. Mind over matter isn't just a phrase. It is a real tool that can aid with his healing."

"You sound like Ryan, my son Adam's wife. She practices holistic healing, has a clinic in Vegas and can probably give more pointers along these lines. I'd like it if you spoke with her about this, too."

"I would love to speak with her."

"Good. I'll let her know." Victoria paused for a moment, then asked, "Do you think he'll walk again?"

"That's a question above my pay grade," Damaris replied with a smile. "With God, all things are possible. I'll pray for Noah's healing, and do everything I can to help him get better."

They chatted a moment longer. When Victoria requested Damaris's cell number, she didn't hesitate. Later, she'd have to examine the deep feelings she felt for her patient, the personal attachment to a positive outcome. She told herself it was because Noah Breedlove was her first solo intake, her first time treating a patient from their time of arrival through departure. It made sense that she'd want to chart the patient's progress, see him through to a successful end. That sounded reasonable, professional even. For now, she'd leave it at that.

A few hours later, Damaris returned to Noah's room. She'd gotten the call that a team from Rehabilitation was on their way over to transfer him. She'd need to make

sure all of his charts were properly updated and ready
to be passed on to the new crew. A sense of anticipation
caused butterflies as she neared his room. The feeling
surprised her and was unnerving, to say the least. Coming from a conservative, religious background, Damaris
had been taught that engagement with the opposite sex
happened largely after marriage. She'd had one serious
boyfriend, Matthew, a church member she'd known since
they were seven and eight years old. At seventeen, when
he was eighteen, they announced their intentions to marry
the following year. Her father didn't consider Matthew
a "good Layman" and was opposed to the union. Eventually he demanded she end the relationship. It was the
first time Damaris had defied her father. They planned
to elope. Before that happened, Matthew was tragically
killed in a motorcycle accident. It had affected her deeply,
both his death and her deception, which is why nearly
five years later, having just turned twenty-three, she was
still unattached…and a virgin.

Even now, the guilt was palpable, with regret worn like
a second skin. Noah was attractive, even with bruises and
scars. But he was also her patient, a depressed, temporarily paralyzed accident victim. And he wasn't a Layman.
She didn't have time for girlie emotions and sternly told
herself to get those errant feelings in check.

She entered his room. The curtains were drawn, the
lights dimmed, Noah's face turned toward the wall. Remembering her advice of keeping the atmosphere around
him as cheery as possible Damaris brightened the lights.

"Wake up, sleepyhead," she sang, while walking over
to the curtains and opening them. "It's moving day."

"Close my curtains," Noah growled. "And get out."

"Sorry, no can do. Your charts have to be updated for

the team on their way to get you. Travis, the physical therapist, is especially excited to get to work with you, get you up and moving as quickly as possible."

Noah snorted. "Yeah, well, good luck with that."

"Luck may play a small role," Damaris continued conversationally, as she checked his blood pressure, temperature and current weight. "But a lot of the improvement will depend on you."

"Here we go, another pep talk." He glared at her. "Save it. I'm not in the mood."

Damaris shrugged her shoulders. "Have it your way."

She said nothing else to Noah but began humming as she continued her work. It was a habit learned from her mother, Bethany, one she did without being aware.

"Will you stop it?" Noah demanded.

Damaris jumped, almost upending her tablet. "Stop what?"

"Singing. Humming. Making noise." He shifted and looked at the ceiling. When he spoke again his voice was calmer but demanding nonetheless. "If you must be here, try to be as invisible as possible, okay?"

Damaris counted to ten, then twenty. She wasn't accustomed to being yelled at, or rude behavior no matter what the injury. She bit her tongue against the desire to tell him just that and focused on finishing up her work as quickly as possible. His presence did funny things to her equilibrium, messed up the status quo and left her wondering about who he was before the accident. What his life was like outside the trauma unit.

"That's it for me, Noah," she said once done. "The guys from Rehab will be here shortly. You'll be transferred to their wing. The nurses I know who work over there are a pretty cheerful bunch," she continued playfully. "So I can't guarantee you'll get the bleak atmosphere you crave, but I believe there will be less humming."

From Noah? Silence, the deafening kind. His stormy countenance could have been cut from stone. Eyes closed. Brow scrunched. Lips set in a hard line. She blocked the desire to step up to his bed and administer a comforting squeeze to his bare, muscled arm or smooth away the creases that the frown created. To Damaris, his facial expression transmitted as pain. She didn't ask about it, and wasn't sure he'd answer anyway. Still, she made an additional note in her report and would be sure to share concerns with the doctor.

"Can I get you anything before I leave?"

"No."

Curt. Final.

"Then let me say it has been my pleasure treating you. I will continue to pray and believe that your body will recover, and that you will be up and walking in no time. Until then, please try to find gratitude in this simple truth. You're alive, which means there is hope."

A huff, as he adjusted his body away from her, a clear dismissal sign. He was right. She was done here and had other patients to see, ones who appreciated her visits and would never silence her hums.

"Goodbye, Noah," she said quietly, then walked out the door, ignoring the fact a part of her heart remained there. Her father would never approve of someone like Noah, who would likely have no real interest in a religious girl like her. The sooner he was out of Manning Valley Medical, the better it would be. For both of them.

Four

Noah wasn't known for angry outbursts, yet he'd had more in the past week than in his entire pre-accident life. Of the four Breedlove brothers, he was the calmest one, the most rational. It wasn't fair to lash out at the nurse. She'd been very patient through his mood swings, all kindness and sunshine when entering the room. Her sunny disposition was part of what irked him, all cheery when he could find no joy. He'd apologized the first time, though not all the way sorry, especially the more he recalled that exchange. Seeing the quiet, almost demure nurse turn into a spitfire made losing his temper almost worth it. Maybe that was why two days after leaving the trauma unit, Damaris was still on his mind.

I wonder what she's like in bed.

Noah banished the unwelcome thought as quickly as it came. As for now, nothing worked below his waist, or may ever function again. His mother told him to stay positive. Ryan said she'd do remote energy work, whatever that was. The angel nurse with the *D* name thought prayers might work and humming would make him feel better. It was all bullshit. From the waist down, he still couldn't move.

"You're alive." That was the parting reason she'd offered him to use as a lifeline. To be grateful because things could be worse. He could have come down from Death Mountain…well…dead. Noah now knew there were worse things than dying, like not being able to lift your leg, or get an erection, or make love again. For a man like him, one who cherished women, that was like not being able to breathe.

A light tap on the door to Noah's private room interrupted his musings. Probably the physical therapist he'd nicknamed Relentless on account of how determined he was to get Noah to move his noodle-like legs.

"Come in."

It wasn't Relentless. It was her. The nurse angel.

"Hello, Noah."

Her smile seemed forced but given their last interaction, commendable. "Hi."

"Remember me?"

"I remember."

"I know, I thought we were done with each other, too." She smiled to show she was joking. "As it turns out, the floor is short-staffed. I'm helping to cover shifts, which means you'll have to put up with me for a couple more days, though I promise not to hum."

"Thank you," he replied, his voice dripping in mock sincerity.

"Ha!"

Damaris began logging his vitals from the monitor into his chart. "How are you doing?"

"Last week I could walk. This week I can't. How do you think I'm doing?"

Her smile faded as quickly as a rainbow. "Still into the pity party, are we? That's not the kind of music I dance to, so I'll leave you to it."

Done with monitoring, she turned to go.

"Wait."

Her hand was on the knob. She didn't turn around, but she didn't open the door, either.

"What's your name again?"

"Damaris. Duh-mare-ess." She turned but made no move to come closer. Instead she leaned against the door. "Friends call me Dee."

"Only friends?"

"Mostly. I make exceptions. Your mother was one."

"Yeah, she's exceptional like that."

The merest hint of a smile flitted across an otherwise serious face.

"Can I call you Dee?"

"Definitely not," Damaris responded to Noah's surprise. "At this time you're still very much in the Damaris category."

Noah smiled.

"Actually," she continued, crossing her arms. "You're almost at the Nurse Damaris point."

His smile broadened. A chuckle almost escaped his mouth. That just happened, when, moments before, Noah wondered if he'd ever laugh again.

"Are you sure about that? If we're going to fight like siblings or arguing lovers, shouldn't we both be on a first-name basis?"

The most delightful shade of red crept from her neck upward. The thought of them being lovers made her blush? She smiled again, more genuine this time. *Ah, there's the sunshine.*

Damaris pushed away from the door and walked toward him. "About what happened the other day…"

"Don't even think about saying you're sorry. I'm the one who owes you an apology. Blowing up at the person trying to help me. Ignoring your presence when you said goodbye. Yours was the appropriate response to someone acting like a total jerk. I'm usually not so combustible. I apologize."

"Your apology is accepted, your mood understood. You're going through a lot."

Noah watched as Damaris approached him. She eyed the various machinery around him as she reached the bed, one especially designed for physical therapy. There were bars and pulleys, with weights on the ends. In the corner was more workout equipment. Beyond the bed was an expanse of window that allowed in abundant natural light along with views of rows of magnificent pine trees and the beautiful mountains of Utah. He saw none of that now, fixated as he was on the beautiful indoor scenery. She had wide, light brown eyes, surrounded by lashes that went on forever. Her nose looked natural, like it hadn't been reduced and sculpted by a knife. Beneath it were lips that were totally kissable, full and luscious, clear gloss-covered temptation. Her hair was thick and curly, her smooth skin the color of a caramel latte. He wondered about her heritage even as he knew it didn't matter. There was nothing to be gained from getting to know her better, except more pain at the thought that talking is probably all they'd ever do.

Damaris checked the intravenous fluid bags. "I see you're still receiving pain medication through the drip. How is your comfort level right now?"

"Better."

"The doctor felt that increasing the dosage would help. I'm glad you're experiencing less pain at least."

She was close enough for him to smell her cologne, something light and fruity, and to notice the slightest spray of freckles across the bridge of her nose. Again, Noah's thoughts turned sensual. He forced them in another direction as Damaris peeked under the bandages on his face.

"Where'd that name come from?"

The fingers lifting the bandages stilled.

"I didn't mean that to sound offensive. It's just that I've never heard it before."

"I get asked that a lot and am not offended at all." She studied his face with an unreadable expression. "Excuse me a moment. Your bandages need changing."

She walked out of the room. Noah's head fell back against the pillow. He'd never been a smooth talker when it came to the ladies, didn't possess his brother Christian's refined mannerisms, Adam's swagger or Nick's charm. He won over women with his intellect. His dark Breedlove good looks and healthy bank account probably didn't hurt, either. He was confident and well-spoken and couldn't figure out why with the nurse angel he was all kinds of verbal fumbles and mental snafus. Then he remembered. The fall on the mountain. Not only his legs had been affected. Something in his brain had jostled loose.

Damaris returned, carrying a small plastic box. She placed the container on a movable tray beside him and removed gauze, astringent and ointment from the container.

For a moment she was quiet, focused on treating his lacerations, the most serious of which was a cut above his right eye. The doctor figured it was from a rock or tree limb hidden just beneath the snow and would leave a scar that only plastic surgery could remove. Her hands were soft, her touch gentle as she began unwinding the soiled gauze from around his head.

"It's from the bible," she said, her voice soft, almost musical.

"Huh?"

"My name. Damaris. It's biblical."

"Oh."

Damaris laughed again. Noah decided he quite liked the sound.

"I gather that's not a book you read often?"

"It's one that I don't read at all."

"Most who do don't remember that name. It's only mentioned once, when the apostle Paul preached the gospel in Athens. She was one of only a few who converted, and as far as we know the only woman."

"So that's why you're named after her, because you're unique?"

"I don't know about me but the name sure is. I think my mom chose it because it was different, something I hated when I was younger."

"Why? I like that it's different."

"I'm a biracial Layman living in Utah."

"You're with the Church of Laymen?" Noah asked the question indifferently, a feat given that the influential religious group was the singular holdout in securing building permits for the biggest project of his professional life.

"Yes. All of the above and a Layman. That's already different enough."

Said in a tone that gave off all kinds of attitude and made him forget why her mere affiliation with his nemesis should squelch the physical attraction. It didn't. Again, Noah noted that flash of fire, a playful spark bursting through the modest image she displayed. He saw it and wondered if her hair was as soft as he imagined, and how wild her curly strands became when released from the band that held them locked at the nape of her neck.

"How'd that happen?"

"Being biracial? It's when two people of different nationalities get together and…"

"Thanks for confirming the details exactly as I imagined them. I was referring to your living in Utah."

"I was born here."

"And being a Layman? I'm not religious and know next to nothing about the church but the little I have read about or seen on television didn't involve people of color."

"There aren't many of us. My dad is a third-generation Layman who went rogue when he met and fell in love with my mom. Initially, his family was staunchly opposed to the union but then they met Bethany."

"Bethany, that's your mom?"

Damaris nodded. "She was a teenager when her family converted to the church. In time she eventually won my father's family over."

"Interesting."

"Quite."

"Any siblings?" Noah asked her, purposely making no mention of his connection to the casino her church opposed. Perhaps something she shared could help him break through the Laymen juggernaut that had proved even more difficult than he and the team had imagined.

The less she knew about his business, the more of hers she might share.

"There are six of us—two boys, four girls."

"You're the oldest?"

"Youngest." Damaris paused. "You look surprised. Do you see a stray gray hair that I don't know about?"

She stretched a curl so that she could see it, feigning concern. And Noah would be damned but there it was again, that feeling he thought was gone forever—joy—subtle yet unmistakable.

"You're beautiful, so no need to worry about that." He watched as that now familiar blush slowly rose from her neck to her cheeks and became even more smitten. There was nothing innocent about the women that Noah dated. As for a woman blushing at hearing a compliment? He hadn't seen that happen in at least ten years.

"I guessed you were the oldest because of the way you take care of me, of all your patients probably, so naturally, like you've been doing it forever. I thought it maybe started when you were a kid, taking care of your brothers and sister."

"No, birds and other animals were my patients. My siblings had to fend for themselves."

"But you became a nurse instead of a veterinarian."

"I love conversing with my patients and don't speak bark or meow."

Noah laughed out loud, another first since the accident, and a rare reaction before then for this serious son.

"What about you?" Damaris asked. "When it comes to the sibling pecking order, where do you fall?"

"The youngest, by fourteen minutes."

"Ah, you're a twin."

"Yes, the fourth of four sons."

"Are you spoiled as is often the case with the youngest child?"

"Definitely not. Are you?"

"Definitely."

They shared another laugh. She was delightful! Her essence remained with Noah long after she'd gone. That all felt amazing. But there was another thought. She was a Layman, part of the church blocking the bill that would green-light the casino project, and costing his investors money with every delay. That didn't feel good at all.

Five

By day five of Noah's hospital stay in Utah, a venerable team of experts had descended to work on his rehabilitation plan. Damaris found herself unexpectedly being one of his rotating nurses, due to a continued shortage of nurses on their ward. She told herself that volunteering to cover after working her shift had nothing to do with Noah. By the time she met Wendy in the cafeteria, she'd almost convinced herself.

They grabbed trays, made their dinner selections and found a table away from other diners. In addition to being her assistant, Wendy was also Damaris's friend. They'd both been so busy working there'd been little time for girl talk, or anything else.

Wendy reached for condiments to dress her burger. "He's gorgeous, isn't he?"

"Who?" Damaris said, shaking the packet of dressing that came with the chicken Caesar salad.

"Who," Wendy parroted. "You know who. The reason you snapped up that extra shift on Rehab. Breedlove. The rich boy."

"I took the extra shift because I could use the money and the floor could use my help."

Wendy chuckled. "Is that the story you're telling yourself? Because I checked you out while he was in trauma and observed something different."

"You observed me doing my job, because that's all that happened."

"What about that day I saw you talking with his mother?"

"I don't discuss patients with their family members?"

"All the time, but you seemed...chattier than with other interactions. Like you were spilling secrets and she was mopping them up."

Damaris shared what she'd told Victoria. "It's what I would have told any family," she finished, sitting back to take a sip of her soda. "The patient is always my focus."

"Calm down, girl. This isn't your employee review. Besides, I don't mind you using the mom to get close to the son. Get him to fall for you and your need of extra shifts will be over!"

"Wendy! I'd never do that."

"I know, and it's a shame. I went online, did a little research. That Noah Breedlove would be quite the catch. His family owns the CANN hotel chain."

Damaris frowned. "The casino?"

"Casinos, plural, housed in some of the most luxurious hotels in the world. Their hotel in Vegas is the only seven-star hotel in North America."

"Hmm."

The information Wendy viewed as exciting, Damaris found troubling as suddenly unrelated pieces of a puzzle now fell into place. His rugged good looks. Being from Nevada. A family able to fly to his bedside at a moment's notice. All of the questions about her faith. Noah Breedlove was a part of the family wanting to do the unthinkable—build a casino in Salt Lake City—something the Church of Laymen would never allow. Is that why he didn't tell her about the connection? Did he know that her father was one of his staunchest opponents? Is that the real reason he apologized for basically being a jerk?

In her faith, money was the root of all evil and gambling a major transgression. Utah, home to the Church of Laymen and where the faith had been birthed in the late nineteenth century, was one of only two states in the entire union where any form of gambling was against the law. Multistate lotteries couldn't muster up enough approval support, largely due to the church's well-lined coffers and powerful political influences. One of those powerful influences was Damaris's father, Franklin. What he lacked in money he made up in machismo. Fanatically devoted to the ministry, he'd campaigned tirelessly against every bill initiated and took pride in "keeping the devil out of the Beehive State."

"Want to hear something even more amazing?" Wendy asked.

Damaris wasn't sure that she did. Didn't matter, as it turned out.

"He has an identical twin named Nick. It's crazy, Dee. They look exactly alike! So—" she lowered her head and her voice "—you go after one, I'll snag the other and we can be sisters-in-law!"

"You know I'm a Layman. I could never go out with Noah, or anyone outside the faith."

Damaris continued to listen as Wendy fairly gushed over all that she'd learned of her patient. She had obviously spent quite a bit of time online researching the Breedloves and was a wealth of information. Over the next fifteen minutes, she went from describing Victoria's role in the CANN Foundation, the charitable arm of the for-profit corporation, to providing each brother's role in the multibillion-dollar enterprise. When Damaris returned to the rehabilitation unit to find Noah's room filled with family, she couldn't help but feel a little bit guilty, like she'd talked about them behind their backs, and, truth be told, been slightly judgmental, too.

"There she is!" Victoria said when Damaris entered. "We were just talking about you."

"All good, I hope." Damaris also hoped the smile she forced carried through in her voice.

"Absolutely," Victoria replied.

She motioned toward a couple looking out the window. The woman broke away and walked over.

"Damaris, this is Ryan, the family's naturopathic doctor I told you about."

Damaris held out her hand. "I find alternative medicine fascinating, Ryan. It's nice to meet you."

"Likewise."

"I told Ryan it would be wonderful if the three of us could have a nice long chat, later, when you're off duty."

"We're short-staffed and very busy," was Damaris's noncommittal reply. "In fact, I really should finish up here and head back over to Trauma."

"Of course," Victoria said. "I'm sorry to have delayed you."

"It's not a problem." And to Ryan. "I'm glad we met."

"Me, too. It would great to talk shop sometime."

Damaris walked over to Noah. "Hello, Noah."

"Hello, Dee."

In spite of her tarnished view of the family, she smiled at his use of her nickname. She also couldn't help but be reminded of Wendy's comment about Noah's appearance and admit he was a very attractive man. His twin, Nick, too, who, without the bruises Noah had sustained in the accident, would be a dead ringer for sure. She stole glances at the clan while performing her duties, her friend's descriptions of each one still fresh in her mind. She looked at the beautiful wives with the handsome husbands and wondered about the type of women in Noah's life. Her mind mulled the possibilities while tending to Noah's rapidly healing wounds.

"Don't bother her, Ryan," Damaris heard Nick saying when she came out of her reverie. "She's focused."

Damaris was totally embarrassed. "I'm sorry, what did you say?"

"When was your last trip to Vegas?"

There was only a second's hesitation before Damaris answered, "I've never been."

The whole room got quiet. Damaris felt the heat of the Breedlove stare.

"You're kidding," Noah's twin brother, Nick, said.

"Never?" Victoria asked.

Ryan looked at the man Damaris assumed was her husband. "Adam, can you believe that?"

Damaris focused on the machine recording Noah's vitals.

"You're a state away from one of the most popular

tourist destinations in America," Victoria continued, "and you've never been there."

"Why not?" Ryan asked.

"The same reason it's taken our project so long to get off the ground here," Noah answered. "She's a member of the single entity blocking the casino being built."

"The Church of Laymen," Nick said, his eyes on Damaris. "She's a part of it."

"Exactly," Noah answered. "The group that wants us to build a hotel and spa only, no gambling."

"If there's no casino, it's not a CANN property," Adam said.

Nicholas, Noah's dad, turned his attention to Damaris. "Since you're a member of that religion, perhaps you can help us understand their zero tolerance for gambling. It's an activity that with the construction of a CANN hotel would boost the economy by more than 25 percent."

Damaris hesitated in giving an answer. While she was clear on the reasons the laws against gambling had been continuously upheld, she didn't want to speak for the church. She opened her mouth to say as much but there was no need. Victoria came to her rescue.

"Oh, no, boys. What we're not going to do is turn Noah's temporary residence into a corporate boardroom. The only focus here should be on helping Noah heal."

"Trust me, wife, him closing this deal would greatly increase that positive attitude you suggested was so important during rehabilitation."

The guys laughed. Damaris smiled. Noah commented, "At just the thought of that deal going through, I feel better already."

Damaris was thankful for Victoria's intervention. It saved her from putting Noah in a very bad mood. Her grandmother had another saying: all money wasn't good money. As long as her father and others like him were on this side of the dirt, there would be no gambling in Salt Lake City, or anywhere in Utah. Period.

Six

Over the next week, Noah met with a group of spinal cord injury specialists, including two on the cutting edge of regeneration research. Because the damaged vertebrae had been crushed, not broken, they thought technology so new it had not yet been announced might work to repair the spine and help him walk again. That the institute was in Denmark gave Noah some concern. But to walk again, he'd travel to Mars.

When he wasn't going through physical therapy or sleeping off the rigorous routines, Noah conducted business on his iPad. His accident had made national news. It was important for his colleagues, employees and investors to know Project Salt Lake was moving forward. He was determined to succeed and driven to quiet the doubters, including his father, who said what he planned could never be done.

That didn't mean the continued delays didn't put a chink or two in his armor. The bill remained stalled within the city council, nowhere close to a vote by the residents. One of the major investors, a financial group based in Dubai, was threatening to pull out. Work kept his mind off his disability, the long road ahead to full recovery and the possibility that as hard as he tried, he may never walk again. For better or worse, focusing on the Salt Lake project also kept his mind on Damaris, a woman who became more off-limits with every facet about her he uncovered. That he didn't question her further after finding out she was a Layman, get deeper insight on the religion and the higher-ups that she knew, was unsettling. Again, he blamed the oversight on the jarring collision his head had with a rock.

When it came to Project Salt Lake, Noah had left the Church of Laymen up to Scott Robinson, a senior advisor on the team. Now, however, he was online doing his own research. He told himself it was because of the church's opposing viewpoints but honestly, it was to learn more about Damaris, too. By the time she arrived in his room an hour later, Noah had learned more than he ever thought he'd know about Laymen, and Damaris was even more an enigma.

"Did you know that until the 1970s, people of color weren't allowed in your church?"

Damaris, who'd barely stepped a toe into the room when the question was hurled, laughed softly. "Good afternoon to you, too."

"Yeah, hi." Noah found the history offensive and felt his question held no humor. "Did you?"

"Somebody's been online, I see." Damaris approached his bed and began her routine. "It's not quite as you've interpreted from whatever you read. People of color could not be ministers or hold leadership positions until the 1970s. But the Church of Laymen has always welcomed everyone."

"In separate services."

"Unfortunately, when the ministry was created, that was the way of life in our country."

As she talked, Noah clicked onto another site, and read from it. "'The Church of Laymen participated in segregated worship services, believing that people of color required a different, simpler form of instruction. Interracial dating was discouraged. Marriage between cultures, forbidden. These rules remained in place until the passing of Wayne Goddard III in 1974. Under new leadership, new policies were adopted and the practice of segregation in all areas of ministry was renounced.'"

Damaris continued her work, checking his vitals and making notations on her chart.

"Well?" he demanded after a pause.

"Well, what?"

"You belong to a church that doesn't even want you in it!"

"That may have been true at one point with some members. But it is not the case today and never was for a majority of the membership. When my mother joined, she was fully accepted."

She took a deep breath. "It is a given that there are areas in our history of which we're not proud. As I've stated, the practices of our church were in line with the times in which it was founded. In the late nineteenth century, segregation was law. As the nation evolved, so did the church."

Damaris made a notation on her tablet. "There's a

slight change in your temperature. Are you feeling differently today than you did yesterday?"

"No."

"No dizziness or nausea?"

"None other than what reading about the history of your church produced."

The slightest of pauses and then she said, "If your symptoms continue, please ring the nurses' station."

Damaris turned to leave. Noah watched her quick retreat, could feel the fire she tried to keep hidden. With eyes like hers, that was impossible. When angry, the light orbs darkened, fairly blazed with the anger she felt. Her jaw had tightened along with her shoulders, before she took a calming breath and responded.

It might have been unfair to attack her in this manner. Neither religion nor politics were subjects for polite company. But the beliefs she and the church members held stood between him, the company's expansion goals and a town's economic well-being. In love, war and business, all was fair.

"Sorry to tell you, Dee, but your church hasn't evolved much."

She spun around, fire in her eyes. "Look, I'm living the life you just read about. No one knows better than me the problems we still face. Even so, the church has made strides in many areas. And while I'm sure it wouldn't seem like it to someone like you, some of the more conservative thinking has been amended."

"Really? Then why is the church still fighting one's right to gamble, a practice that is legal in forty-eight other states? Or even something as simple as buying a lottery ticket, something residents in forty-four other states can do? Why has it taken two years for our company to even have a member from your ministry sit at the bargaining table?"

"Because gambling is built on greed and gluttony," Damaris responded, anger beginning to leak through her professional facade. "And while it is my understanding that your family has lots of it, loving money is the root of all evil. People who crave it suffer and have no true faith."

Indignation caused Noah to lift his head off the pillow. "Money is evil? So you're working for free?"

"Right now, I'm not working at all. I'm arguing with you. But that's about to change."

She whirled around again, yanked open the door and stormed from the room. For a few seconds Noah stared at the door, as the electricity of their exchange continued to swirl around him. He flopped back, spent yet exhilarated. There was nothing like a good verbal joust to get the blood flowing. In Breedlove boardrooms that happened quite often. Heated arguments. Passionate debates. For the first time since he entered this place on a stretcher, Noah felt more like himself. He didn't need legs to hold his own in an intellectual conversation. Reinvigorated, Noah opened a Word document on his tablet and began writing a memo to his team. Damaris had relit his passion, stoked his determination. Building, winning, the Breedlove way; failure never an option. When it came to the CANN Casino Hotel and Spa being built in Utah, the fight was far from over. As for the conversation with Damaris about the Church of Laymen, or conversing in general, Noah wasn't finished there, either.

Seven

Damaris chided herself all the way back to Trauma, couldn't believe how she'd lost her temper and allowed herself to be goaded into a quarrel. Above all else, Noah was a patient. He deserved to be treated with compassion and care. What Noah thought about the church was of no concern, though his prodding questions raised her own. What his company did or didn't do with their casino hotels was none of her business, either. That was her father's arena. What did it matter anyway? In a couple days, Noah Breedlove and his wealthy family would leave the hospital where Damaris worked, she'd never see them again and the crazy feelings that bubbled up every time she saw the handsome heathen would quickly go away.

Two days later, Damaris sat at her desk trying to focus. She'd accessed Noah's files in the system and knew he was being discharged within the hour. For the best, Damaris told herself, then tried to believe it. From the first time their eyes met, her mind had been screwy. She'd even stooped to going online and learning more about him and his family. Everything Wendy had told her was true, and was just the tip of the iceberg. The pictures of them were glamorous, the guys looking decadent in full tuxedos, the girls hobnobbing with celebrities and sports superstars. Despite being a sensible, low-key kind of girl, she'd still sat back and wondered how it was to live like the rich and famous. To have everything you needed at your fingertips, where you could buy whatever you wanted. It was fanciful imaginings with no value whatsoever. With him back in Las Vegas, she could stop fantasizing and resume her conservative, predictable life.

She'd just begun a report for Dr. Noble when her intercom sounded. "Dee?"

Damaris pressed a button. "Hey, Wendy."

"Someone's here to see you. A…Mrs. Breedlove."

"Umm…okay. Can you escort her to the office? We'll be able to have a more private discussion in here."

"Sure thing."

Damaris disconnected the call, quickly opened her desk drawer and pulled out a rarely used compact and a tube of pale pink gloss. When the door opened, which missus would she see? Her first thought was Victoria, but she had Damaris's cell number. What could be so important that instead of calling, she'd come over in person?

Damaris stood as Victoria walked into the office, looking casually sophisticated in navy slacks with a matching tunic. Her short black bob was stylishly streaked with gray, and accented a flawlessly made up heart-shaped face. She wore a matching pearl earring and necklace set and stylish bone-colored heels. Damaris knew from

Noah's chart that he was twenty-five, and from an earlier conversation that he and his twin brother were the youngest of four sons. That meant Victoria had to be in her fifties. Yet Damaris swore she didn't look a day over thirty-five.

"Hello, Victoria." She held out her hand.

Victoria grasped it with one hand and covered it with the other. "I was afraid that with it being a Saturday you'd be off work. I'm glad to have this opportunity to chat in person."

Damaris's curiosity was instantly aroused. Something was on Victoria's mind.

"Please, have a seat." Instead of returning to the seat behind her desk, Damaris sat in one of two matching chairs on the opposite wall. Victoria sat in the other one, a magazine-strewn table between them.

"Can I get you something to drink? Coffee, tea or a water?"

"No, thank you," Victoria said with a glance around the small office. "I'm fine."

Clearly not, Damaris thought, the way Victoria was wringing her hands.

"I understand Noah is scheduled to leave today. Have they already checked him out?"

"No, but he'll be ready to leave soon and frankly, Damaris, I'm terrified."

"That's completely understandable, Victoria. If I were a mother, my feelings would be the same. Noah appears to be a determined man, one who can accomplish anything on which he sets his mind and intention. As he gets better physically, his mood will improve."

"He's always been a brooder," Victoria explained. "The quietest of my children by far. He says he's okay, but he fears for his future. He's always enjoyed a very active lifestyle. This is a huge change."

Damaris's heart went out to Victoria. She could read worry all over the mother's face.

"I wish I could offer assurances for exactly how all this turns out or guarantee that he'll walk again. The truth is, all of you are facing unknown, uncharted territory. Uncertainty is scary. But from what I've seen, Noah has a strong support system, starting with you and the close-knit family you've created. He's got a team of international specialists charting his medical progress. It will be daunting and seem impossible at times. But you're a strong woman. You can do this."

"I hope so," Victoria whispered, her eyes bright with unshed tears. "If it were possible to switch places with him, I'd do it in a heartbeat."

Damaris reached over and placed a comforting hand on her arm. "Look, this isn't something I normally do, but you have my number. If you ever want to talk about the residue left over from his traumatic injuries, the rehabilitation process or just someone who believes it is possible for your son to get better, please give me a call."

"That's very kind of you, Damaris."

"Noah was my first intake as lead nurse on the trauma ward—a memorable experience. I'm happy to help."

"I believe you mean that."

"I do, absolutely."

"Well, I felt it out of place to ask this, but since you volunteered your continued assistance, there is one something you could do that would ease my worries considerably and I think help Noah, too."

"What's that?"

"Continue to help with his recovery."

"I'd gladly help if that were happening here, but as I understand it he's being released to the care of a team in Las Vegas, correct? And that Travis will be going with him."

"All of that's true. A brand-new duplex is being built, along with a customized rehabilitation workout room nearby to help Noah improve as quickly as possible."

"You built a whole house that quickly, in the short time that Noah's been here?"

"A whole two houses," Victoria said with a smile. "It took pulling in favors, a top-notch construction company and a small army working around the clock to pull it off. But my Noah has already been through so much. I wanted him to come home to a place where he could feel comfortable, somewhat independent, a place designed to meet his new set of needs. I get the feeling, though, that my son's mental and emotional recovery is as or more important than the physical aspect. You're a great nurse, Damaris, kind and compassionate and highly skilled. I've met a lot of people and can read them very well. I would love to have you as part of the team assembled on my son's behalf."

Damaris was stunned into silence, trying to absorb a request she couldn't possibly have heard.

"I don't see how that could be possible."

"You'd have to relocate, of course," Victoria said with a smile. "We'd match whatever salary and benefits the hospital pays you," she continued, leaving no doubt that indeed a job offer had just been made.

"And take care of the relocation, along with providing room and board."

The only reason Damaris didn't fall over was because she was already sitting down.

"You're asking me to move to Vegas?"

"It's a big ask but yes, for Noah. He's very sensitive about his…condition. But you were here from the beginning. He responds well to your treatment and care. He's talked about you when you're not around, how you've encouraged him and helped him believe that he could get better."

"He has?"

Victoria nodded. "That's surprising?"

"Absolutely. The reactions I've seen aren't ones very receptive to messages on the power of positive thinking. In fact… I just… Have you talked to Noah about this?"

"I wanted to ask you first. I didn't want to get his hopes up and then have them dashed if you can't accept the offer."

"You might want to run it by him. I'm not sure he'd want me on the team."

"Why not?"

"I'm a Layman, Victoria, part of the group opposing his casino plans. My views line up on the side of the church. I don't believe in gambling, either."

"I don't plan to put such in your job description."

"You'd still want me to work for you, given my position?"

"Absolutely. I want to do whatever it takes to help my son heal."

"I'm floored, honestly, and don't know what to say."

"Then say nothing. Think about it and give me an answer in a couple days. Oh, and please know that money is no object. If doubling the salary will help make your decision easier, then consider it done."

"Wow. I can't believe what you've just offered. It's a lot to think about."

"I know, dear, and I don't mean to push. But it's my son's life and emotional well-being on the line. I want to do everything possible to help him recover as quickly and completely as he possibly can."

Damaris walked Victoria to the elevator. Wendy followed her back.

"What was that about?"

Damaris closed the door, leaned against it and put her hands over her eyes. "I don't believe what just happened."

"What? Oh my gosh, Dee, spill it!"

"Promise you won't breathe a word of this to anyone?"

"Promise."

There was no chance of anyone overhearing but Damaris lowered her voice anyway.

"Victoria just offered me a job."

"What?" Wendy squealed.

"Shh!"

"Sorry." Wendy adjusted her voice to an exaggerated whisper. "What?"

Damaris appreciated her friend's humor. It took away some of her angst.

"Victoria asked if I'd relocate to Las Vegas and become her son's personal nurse."

"Stop lying."

"Cross my heart."

"Oh my gosh, Dee! That's amazing! When are you leaving?"

"What do you mean, leaving? I can't accept that job."

"You can't not take it. Living in Las Vegas as that hunk's personal nurse? It's the job of a lifetime! There's no telling what working with them could lead to, but it would definitely be something you couldn't get here. Don't you remember what I told you about that family?

How they own a huge hotel chain and have properties all over the world? Don't be stupid, Damaris. It's a wonderful opportunity, plus they have more money than God!"

She didn't tell Wendy, who would surely berate her, but for Damaris, that was part of the problem. The other was her father. He'd absolutely hit the roof. To him, Las Vegas was akin to Sodom and Gomorrah, two biblical cities given over to debauchery and eventually destroyed with fire and brimstone. Could she move to such a place and stay true to her faith? The other question was did she want to?

Eight

He'd always loved the family estate, hundreds of acres encircled by mountains. Some landscaped, some wild, all beautiful. But the man who left two weeks ago wasn't the one who returned. That self-assured powerhouse no longer existed yet Breedlove, Nevada, a town cofounded by his father, and this, the land that was embedded in his DNA, hadn't changed. It still felt like home. Now, a day after arriving, he was trying to adjust to his new digs, an architectural miracle performed by an award-winning construction company and over a hundred hired hands. He was still checking out the four-thousand-foot, wheelchair-accessible wonder when the phone rang. He wheeled himself over to where he'd left both his business and personal cell phones on the table. He picked up the one for personal use and saw a number he didn't recognize.

"Noah Breedlove."

"Hi, Noah. It's Damaris."

His heartbeat increased. She didn't have to say her name. He'd know that voice anywhere.

"Your Manning Valley trauma nurse."

Only then did he realize he hadn't yet spoken.

"There's probably only one Damaris in this country, remember? I know who you are."

"Oh, okay. Good. How's it going, Noah? How are you adjusting to your new life?"

"How'd you get my number?"

"Your mother asked me to give you a call."

"Figures," he mumbled.

"If this is a bad time…"

"No, it isn't."

Noah's reaction was from knowing that Victoria Breedlove was a notorious matchmaker, always trying to line up the next wedding celebration. She'd been successful with his brothers Christian and Adam. She also possessed the uncanny ability to see romance blooming before the sons knew it had been planted. Noah had no intentions of continuing her winning streak with Damaris or anyone else.

"I know it's only been a few days," Damaris continued. "Which has probably been filled with a myriad of ways in which you're readjusting."

"That's an understatement. Everything is different. Almost every single thing I've ever done in life."

"I can't imagine."

Noah realized how good it felt to be sharing his feelings with someone who not only cared but, because of her profession, could possibly understand what he was going through better than most.

"Have you worked with other paralyzed patients?"

"Not in the capacity of a professional nurse. When in college, however, there was a little boy whom I studied with. His name was Trevor. He'd been paralyzed in a terrible freak accident where the industry-standard tractor his father used on their family farm malfunctioned when his dad put it in Drive and the machine went in Reverse. Trevor was standing behind it. His legs were crushed. It was horrific, to say the least. His family marveled that he lived, and even more at his spirit coming out of the chaos."

"Let me guess, his positive attitude," Noah replied, sarcasm dripping off the words.

"Not so much positive, as grateful. He was only seven years old at the time, nine now. But his perspective was so far beyond his years, very mature. He was happy to still be alive."

"Are you still in touch with him?"

"I am."

"Do you make it a practice of staying in touch with all of your patients?"

"No. Trevor is the only one."

"So, how did my mother convince you to call me?"

"She offered me a job."

Oh, here we go. Noah rolled his eyes. That was how she'd gotten her firstborn down the aisle.

"What could you do for me here?"

"Be a part of your medical team, same as when you were at Manning Valley."

Noah was shocked but not surprised. Many looking on would assume that their father, Nicholas, was where the Breedlove brothers got all their negotiation skills. That was true, in part. But calculated strategizing? That was all Victoria. The Breedlove family was her chessboard. She played for all to win.

"What do you think about that?" he finally asked.

"Not much, to be honest."

Her brutally forthright answer was refreshing. "Damn, girl. Say it like you mean it."

"I'm sorry. That wasn't meant to come off as a harsh statement. It's just that…"

Noah wheeled around so that he could see the home's perfectly landscaped backyard. A white peacock, part of a flock that roamed the Breedlove estate, strutted across the concrete surrounding the infinity pool. Once again, he was enjoying the verbal exchange with Damaris. He tried not to notice the way talking with her excited him.

"Go on."

"There are so many reasons I can't accept your mother's offer. Moving away from home and to Las Vegas of all places. Your company's stance on gambling, which is diametrically opposed to the faith that I practice. And yet…"

"Continue," he softly encouraged her. He watched as the sun began to sink behind a tall mountain as if it, too, was in line with setting a certain mood.

"Thinking of the offer from a practical and career-driven standpoint, it is certainly one that shouldn't be turned down outright. I'd work alongside some of the world's preeminent leaders in treating paralysis, and on the cutting edge of new technology to aid one's road back to a more normal way of life."

She paused, and Noah could imagine her actions. How she set her shoulders a certain way when needing mental reinforcement. He remained quiet, as he often did in business negotiations, where silence was often golden, and timing paramount.

"There's one very big problem, however," she said.

"And that is?"

"You."

"Me?"

"Us. Our last meeting didn't end on the best of terms."

"I'm sorry to have frightened you."

"Frightened? Excuse me? When did you think I was scared?"

"When you used being at work as an excuse to run away from our discussion."

"Being the youngest, you should know we never run away…from anything."

"Then you're considering my mother's offer?"

"Are you sure you want me to? I'm an überpositive, humming, religious nurse whose stance on gambling is not likely to change."

"And sometimes I can be an asshole. That's not likely to change soon, either. Plus, I'm going to keep fighting to build my casino. Given that knowledge, are you sure you want the job?"

"I probably shouldn't," she replied.

"Knowing Mom, I'm sure it's a generous and more than fair offer, so why not? Unless you're afraid."

"I thought you'd had enough of me here in Utah. I am sure there are any number of qualified nurses in Vegas, ones who love gambling and are ready to feed your ego in the quest to put slot machines all over the world."

"CANN International is about more than gambling."

"Prove it."

Now it was Noah's turn to get clarification. "Excuse me?"

"You said that part of the reason your company was fighting for a hotel in Salt Lake was to boost the economy, right?"

"That's correct." Noah sat straighter in his chair. Where was she going with this?

"Why can't you do that without the casino, with your company erecting a nongambling hotel and spa?"

"Because that is not the CANN brand, darling, an aspect of business I doubt you know much about. Your area of expertise is healing bodies. Mine is building casino hotels. I think this conversation will go much better if we stay in our perspective lanes."

"Agreed. That said, I'll let Victoria know that I can't take the position. I wish you well."

"That's no surprise. Only the best of the best can navigate our family's dynamics, and my specific set of challenges. Those who are weak in any area of their makeup need not apply, especially someone who lets an organization think for them instead of figuring out life on their own."

"Excuse me?"

"You heard me."

The response he received was a click and then silence. Damaris had hung up on him. Good. The last thing he needed was a gorgeous Goody Two-shoes around, one with soft curly hair his fingers itched to touch and a pair of eyes he could get lost in, though a little part of his heart had lightened at the thought of her coming to Vegas. He was focused on two things, walking and getting the casino bill passed, and not necessarily in that order. Anything else was a distraction, especially the angel named Dee.

Nine

Of all the pompous, arrogant, self-righteous posturing. The unmitigated gall! Damaris paced her room, about to burn a hole in the carpet of the upstairs room she'd called home for seventeen years before going to college and for the year since she'd graduated with a nursing degree. Who was he to insinuate that she was afraid to take the job? That she couldn't handle, what did he call it? Putting herself out there. How dare he suggest that she was a blind follower of faith unable to think for herself.

Damaris stopped, tapped the face of her phone and scrolled to Victoria's number. "I don't need to put up with this drama," she mumbled to herself as she pressed Victoria's number to make the connection.

Drama. Trauma.

Damaris hurriedly ended the call. The realization of the truth behind Noah's words hit her squarely between the eyes. She eased down on the bed, as the weight of the intuitive revelation settled on her heart. Noah's antics had nothing to do with her. His blustering was covering up what was really going on inside him. Fear. Not hers, his. Noah was the one who was afraid. Who wouldn't be? The world as he knew it had exploded. He'd landed unable to move his legs and didn't know if he'd do so again.

He landed in my care for a reason.

Damaris looked around the room, though the thought came from somewhere deep inside her. She went into nursing to help people get better, especially those dealing with trauma. Noah's experience was the sum total of all she'd learned, someone deeply troubled by an experience that had changed his world's paradigm. In that instant, what she needed to do became crystal clear. She again tapped a number on her cell phone, quickly, before she could think about what she was doing and change her mind.

"Damaris?"

Hearing her name caused an already rattled Damaris to search for words. "Um, yes, hi, Victoria."

"I recognized your number by the area code. You're my only Utah contact. Did you call just a moment ago?"

"Yes, that was me. I thought I disconnected the call before it went through."

"That's quite all right. I'm glad you called and hope it's to tell me you've accepted my job offer."

"Yes, I was calling to tell you that I'd take the job, though I'm not sure I should."

"Because of the gambling issue?"

"Because I just hung up on my patient."

Victoria laughed, much to Damaris's surprise. "I can guarantee you that doesn't happen too often. Did Noah deserve to be let go without a goodbye?"

"Given that I don't like being insulted, it was either that or say something that couldn't be taken back."

"Then good for you. I agree that it's exactly what you should have done. Now, I'll have my new assistant, Farrah, send over the employment agreement."

"Perhaps you should speak with Noah before we finalize this arrangement."

"I'll handle Noah. Meanwhile, please review the agreement carefully as it is legally binding. You've got what he needs—a determined attitude. Your arrival will be a perfect surprise."

Over the next several minutes, Damaris and Victoria ironed out the details of her employment, which would fall under a division of CANN International. Damaris voiced her discomfort in being connected to a business known for gambling. Victoria understood her concerns but assured her that wasn't a problem.

"Breedlove, Nevada, is twenty minutes and a world away from Vegas," Victoria assured her. "You'll live in an area where there is not a slot machine in sight."

Within hours, an agreement had been faxed over for Damaris's perusal and signature. Victoria wanted her to start right away. For her, having Damaris arrive the next day would have been preferable. But knowing the hospital was already short-staffed, Damaris gave her superiors a two-week notice and the promise to assist in finding her replacement. Before putting in her notice, she told Wendy. Her friend was ecstatic.

"Your whole world is about to change," she assured Damaris with a big bear hug. "Don't go all bright lights, big city and forget about us little people."

Telling her parents was going to be the hard part. Her father was an official consultant to the city council, and sure to know the Breedlove name. He'd object to her working for owners of a gambling enterprise or, worse, forbid her from leaving. Not wanting to again blatantly defy him, Damaris crafted a story that would not include the total truth but was not an outright lie, either. That night, during dinner, she broached the subject.

"I've taken a new job," she casually began, with her heart about to beat out of her chest.

"So soon?" her mother, Bethany, responded. "You were just assigned as head nurse in the trauma department. Where are they moving you?"

"It's not at Manning Valley Medical," Damaris said.

This piqued her father's interest. "They have the best trauma unit in the state. It's where you wanted to work."

"It is and I'm grateful to have been hired there. In fact, that position is what has led to an offer too good to refuse. I'll be working as a private nurse for a recent paraplegic, making twice what I'm making now and with similar benefits. I'll have to relocate for the position, but those expenses will be covered as part of the employment package."

"To where?" Franklin asked.

"Nevada." Damaris was careful not to say Las Vegas. Mentioning the state was tricky enough.

"Las Vegas?" Her father spat out the words she'd dared not utter.

"Oh, no," she hastily replied. "I made my stance on gambling very clear at the onset and was assured that where the patient lives, and where I'll reside, is far from that world."

"Nevada isn't a big enough state for it to be that far. Are they Laymen?" Franklin asked.

"No, but I've already gone online and found out that

there is a church I can attend about ten minutes away. Have you ever visited the church in Nevada, Dad?"

"It's been years since I've stepped foot in Nevada but yes, I was there for that church's inaugural celebration. The pastor's name is Dean Sullivan. You know his grandfather, Pastor Joseph Sullivan, whose legacy goes all the way back to the founding members of our church."

Just great. Someone who intimately knows my father. While keeping that thought to herself, she said, "I saw that on the website and thought his name sounded familiar. He looks to have a lovely family—two boys and two girls."

"I think moving to a new location and a new congregation will be good for you," Bethany offered. "I'm sure there are fine young men in Pastor Sullivan's congregation. Ones who will get you thinking about marriage and starting your own family."

Damaris was glad the conversation shifted away from the Breedloves but not comfortable with its new direction. Especially since the face that sprang up when her mom mentioned marriage belonged to the handsome man about to be her sole patient. So what if even injured he radiated with confidence and swagger? Who cared if he was successful and ridiculously wealthy as Wendy had shared? None of it mattered, especially that. She was a Layman. He wasn't. He'd probably had sex. She hadn't. His family built casinos. Her family blocked them. They were polar opposites with only one thing in common—a desire to see Noah recover as quickly and fully as possible. She had two weeks to resolve any wayward feelings to the contrary once and for all. Over the days that followed she'd come to realize she needed every second.

The two weeks flew by in a whirlwind of packing, planning and searching for her replacement. Damaris was relieved when a nurse who'd recently relocated from the East Coast and had more than twenty years' experience sent in her résumé. She was interviewed that very afternoon and hired the next day. In between packing, there were several calls between Damaris and Victoria, who'd scheduled a meeting with Noah's team of caretakers the morning following her arrival. It was the first time Damaris would live outside her home state. The emotions she felt surprised her. However, with a farewell dinner that included her siblings, their spouses and friends from church, the Sullivans' phone number recorded in her phone and an admonition from her father to be at their church that Sunday, Damaris was dropped off at the airport the next day by her mother and boarded a flight into the unknown.

"Yo! Anybody home?"

Noah heard the front door open. "Where else would I be?" he yelled.

He reached the foyer just as Adam turned the corner. His brother removed his signature Stetson and brushed grass off his boots.

"You rode Thunder over."

"Yes, and realized there's something I need to add to your driveway. A hitching post."

"Great," Noah mumbled. "Yet another reminder of something else I can't do."

"Something you can't do today," Adam said. "From the looks of the physical therapist you hired away from Utah, the situation could look different as early as tomorrow."

Noah wheeled around and headed toward the kitchen. Adam followed him. "How's he working out?"

"Travis? He's cool. Strong enough to help do what I can't do myself. Missing a sympathy gene, which works in his favor."

Adam accepted the bottle of beer that Noah offered. "I heard that." He unscrewed the top and took a healthy swallow. "What else is going on?"

"Besides assembling the team to help put me back together? Not much."

"How's that going?"

"Mom's pretty much in charge. She hired a nurse who'll work closely with Travis and be a liaison to the specialists and the staff at the institute."

"I've heard the Nevada Institute of Medicine has some of the best. Still, it's too bad you couldn't get that PYT from the hospital in Utah."

Noah knew Damaris was the pretty young thing to whom Adam referred. "It's just as well. She's too holy for the likes of this place."

"Right, a Layman. That was a surprise."

"Why?"

Adam shrugged. "I guess I assumed that the women in a church like that would be wearing long dresses and bonnets."

"Maybe she does," Noah mumbled sarcastically.

"She could wear a burlap sack and still turn heads."

"Hey! Whose side are you on?"

Adam raised his hands. "Sorry, bro. Just saying. Hey, did you talk to her about Project Salt Lake? Maybe it's just the old guard resisting. Maybe Dee and the younger members could be the bridge between sides."

"That would be a negative, my good man. She doesn't

want the casino, either. Believes the project should move ahead as just a hotel and spa."

"Damn! We're so close! You and the team have gone further than any of us imagined. When the mayor came on board…"

"He brought the rest of the business community with him. The Church of Laymen is our last holdout."

"And you've got how long to change their minds?"

"Probably not long enough. The council is going to choose a date at their next meeting—a special session to vote on this issue alone."

"Then I guess you're right."

"About what?"

"Dee the Layman not being the right nurse for you. Still won't hurt if whoever Mom finds is attractive. I think a sexy nurse is like a spoonful of sugar."

Noah cocked a brow.

"You know, helps the medicine go down."

"That was really lame," Noah deadpanned.

"True, though," Adam replied.

"Given what Travis told Mom, it will probably be a dude. He's got some business to handle on the East Coast in the next two weeks that will take him away for several days."

"What does that have to do with who'll be your nurse?"

"The physical capacity to help me do what until now I took for granted—walk, bathe, dress, stuff like that."

"Sorry, bro," Adam said with a hand on his brother's shoulder.

"Don't worry about it," Noah responded. "It is what it is."

Damaris thought she'd prepared herself to enter rich man's land. Wrong. As a set of massive wrought-iron gates opened and the car journeyed down a smoothly paved road surrounded by meticulously landscaped beauty, she realized two things. The pictures online of the Breedlove mansion did not do it justice and there was a level of rich beyond what she'd imagined. She wondered about the people who lived in what was described to her as a subdivision of Breedlove, Nevada, architectural wonders that sat on huge plots of land on appropriately named streets like Ace of Diamonds Alley and Royal Flush Road. As she worked to take in all that they passed—grazing horses, strutting peacocks, cows dotting the landscape behind what looked like a ranch—they turned into the circular drive of a stately mansion that appeared large enough to be a hotel. Damaris watched as the front door opened and Victoria walked out to greet her.

"Damaris!"

She stepped out of the car and into Victoria's welcoming embrace. "Welcome to Breedlove!"

Victoria hooked her arm in Damaris's and began walking them toward the door. "Don't worry about your bags. They'll be deposited at your new home. I hope you're hungry. I understand Noah's personal chef, Jermaine, has put together a scrumptious meal. In a bit, we'll head there for lunch. He's a new hire and I can't wait to try his food. Goodness! Listen to me ramble." Victoria took Damaris's hand and squeezed it. "I'm just so glad you're here."

They'd stepped through a set of ornately designed double doors and into a massive foyer straight off a Hollywood movie soundstage. The floor was slate tile. The ceiling was at least twenty feet high, dominated by a chandelier with a value that Damaris guessed probably exceeded some country's GNP. It was all she could do not to drop her jaw and gawk like a country bumpkin.

"How was your flight?"

"Thankfully, uneventful." They reached a hallway beyond which were paneless windows that showcased an expansive backyard. "Your home is stunning."

"Thank you. Making it and then keeping it that way is an ongoing labor of love."

They tied up a few loose ends regarding Damaris's employment, such as clarifying work hours and the days she'd have off. Victoria invited her to freshen up in the guest bath before they piled into her brand-new custom Escalade for the short drive to Noah's home. Again, Damaris was struck by the size and splendor of the homes that dotted the countryside. Before she had the chance to inquire about these neighbors, however, Victoria pulled into a driveway.

"Noah has no idea you've been hired," Victoria said, her eyes gleaming mischievously. "I can't wait to see his reaction."

"You didn't tell him?" Damaris wasn't sure surprising him was the best idea.

"No, but he'll be happy with my choice. Trust me," Victoria said, as she reached for the door handle. "A mother knows."

They walked up a ramp leading to a wide wraparound porch.

"Noah!" Victoria sang out, as she reached for the door. "Where are you? I'm with the newest member of your team!"

"In the dining room, Mom. Ready to dig into this feast that's..."

As Victoria came around the corner with Damaris in tow, his words died.

"Hello, Noah," Damaris said in a voice lighter and softer than she'd intended.

"Dee," he replied, his face devoid of emotion. "What are you doing here?"

Ten

Great. Just what he needed. Noah laid down his fork and plopped back in the chair—his appetite fleeing along with his smile. He'd spent the better part of the morning debating those with her mindset, people who felt it was their right—no, duty—to determine how and where other adults spent their money. And here one comes, invited by his mother no less, right through his front door.

"I asked you a question," Noah said. "Why—"

"Please, forgive my son's lack of manners," Victoria interrupted, gesturing toward a cushioned seat while seamlessly gliding over the awkward moment. "You remember Damaris, darling, from Manning Valley Medical."

"I remember the Layman," he snapped. "The one who'd never before been to Nevada. It's still Sin City," he taunted. "Do you think anything's changed?"

"I was hoping you had," Damaris calmly replied,

meeting his steely gaze with her own. "It is clear there is more work to do."

"And you think you're the one to do it?" He asked this in the same brusque tone, even though inwardly he thought her flippant reply was sexy as hell.

"Victoria does."

Victoria reached for a pitcher of lemony tea and began filling their glasses. "I met with an agency, Noah, and considered their recommendations. In my opinion, Dee's attributes will best complement the rest of the team and lead to what we all want, for you to fully recover."

Noah reached for his glass, his eyes on Damaris. "What do you think?"

"I've studied hard, worked harder and am confident in my skills. But the team and I are only half of the equation. The other half involves desire, determination, attitude, belief. I think those intangibles as much as any medical procedure go a long way to aiding recovery. Can you walk again? I think so. But will you, and how long will that take? That, I think, is entirely up to you."

The room fell silent, even as a tension heightened by mutual attraction fairly crackled in the air.

After a moment, Victoria asked, "Well, Noah, do you agree that Dee will be an asset to your medical team?"

"I do," he replied, somewhat begrudgingly. "Just can't believe she accepted your offer."

"Your mom drives a hard bargain," Damaris said, as she took the tongs Victoria offered and placed a helping of beef on her plate.

Offered a lot of that evil money, he wanted to say, but held his tongue. Before starting another argument, no matter how stimulating, he needed to at least wait until her bags were unpacked.

Victoria lifted the lid of a serving bowl, releasing the fragrant aroma of roasted vegetables with the steam. "I was quite persistent," she admitted.

"You didn't have to be."

Noah placed a freshly baked roll on a saucer and reached for the herb butter beside it. At her answer, his hand stilled.

"This is a rare and unique opportunity to work with specialists who are at the top of their fields. I can learn so much during the time that I'm here, then apply that knowledge while working with other trauma patients when I return to Manning Valley Medical or wherever I'm hired."

He resumed eating, chagrined that his thoughts had drifted toward the impossible. What did he think Damaris was going to say? That she found him attractive, and came here to date? That they were fresh out of gamblers, not to mention paraplegics, in Utah so she thought to give this Breedlove a shot?

"Damaris has already provided valuable input regarding your overall treatment," Victoria was saying when Noah tuned back in. "Over the past week, she and Travis have begun mapping out a game plan that will coincide with what's done at the rehab center and through the doctor's recommendations."

Noah was stunned. "You were hired over a week ago?" No answer. "What else have you two been plotting behind my back?"

"Only the plan to get you better," Victoria answered, after finishing a bite. "Which will have to include a good amount of exercise if Jermaine keeps fixing meals as delicious as this one. Don't be shy," she said to Damaris. "Help yourself to more food."

"Everything's delicious. I've never eaten such tender beef."

"Repeat that the next time you're around Adam," Noah said. "You'll become his friend for life."

Over a lunch filled with some of the best foods Damaris had tasted, the three put Noah's health aside and chatted on more casual topics. Victoria and Noah plied Damaris with tales of growing up in Breedlove's Wild West, with Sin City in the background. Damaris shared being raised in a conservative enclave where life revolved around church and family. Noah was amazed at Damaris's lack of knowledge when it came to pop culture, from popular music and video games to the latest blockbuster films. He was equally impressed of her love for the outdoors; how her family camped, hunted and went skiing on a regular basis. Noah could tell Damaris was initially nervous and liked how she grew more animated the more she relaxed.

Lunch ended with a light dessert of strawberries and vanilla cream over shortcake biscuits. Shortly after the last forkful, Victoria looked at her watch.

"I have a foundation meeting before Nicholas and I leave for a dinner engagement. Noah, would you be kind enough to give Dee a tour of her home, and make sure she gets settled in for the night?"

"That's no problem."

She turned to Damaris. "Your pantry is stocked, and Noah's new chef, Jermaine, has placed a couple days' supply of fresh frozen dishes in your freezer. We didn't know if you cooked or not and wanted to make sure you didn't starve."

"I do cook but it's nice to have something already prepared."

"Breakfast at the main house is at eight. You're welcome to join us. Our meeting begins at nine in the same place we met earlier."

Victoria said her goodbyes and sailed out of the room.

"Well," Damaris began, watching her exit, "were you really as shocked as you sounded when I walked into the room?"

"Even more than that." Noah began wheeling himself from the room. Damaris followed him. "You had my number. Why didn't you call?"

"I'd already given notice at Manning Valley Medical and didn't want to take the chance of getting fired barely after being hired."

"Ha! Can't say I blame you. Given our last few conversations, that chance was real."

"Exactly."

"Even though during our last conversation, as I recall, you hung up on me."

"As I remember it, the call got disconnected."

"Yeah, by your finger."

Damaris suppressed a smile. "Perhaps."

Damaris admired the furnishings as they passed through the living room and down the hall to the front door. Unlike the main house clearly stamped with Victoria's signature, this decor was simple, masculine, a blending of rustic and modern that Damaris guessed was quite like the man who lived here. She assumed the van outside was wheelchair accessible and that was what they'd be driving to her home. Instead of heading down the ramp as she'd almost done, Noah continued down the length of the porch to another front door that mirrored the one she'd just closed.

Noah stopped his chair just to the left of the entrance. "Welcome to your new home."

Damaris's eyes flared briefly. "My home?"

"Yes."

"I'm staying here?"

Noah nodded. "This is a duplex. The architects did a brilliant job of disguising that fact."

Damaris worked to process Noah's simple revelation, to juxtapose it over the humble abode she'd imagined would be hers as part of the Breedloves' household staff. She tried to hide her shock but judging from the smirk on Noah's face, she wasn't totally successful. Shock gave way to mortification at what her family would think of her living arrangement. That she would be a single woman living alone, next door to a single man. Any normal person would conclude that a man paralyzed from the waist down posed no sexual threat to his daughter but for Laymen there were sins that could be done with one's hand. Or mouth. Or mind. She was about to voice an objection when another thought occurred. Surely this entire place wasn't for her. She hadn't considered that the entire staff would share quarters but given the size it shouldn't be a problem.

"Do Travis and your chef live here, too?"

"No, Dee. This is all yours." Damaris stood staring at the still-closed door. "Unlike mine, this door isn't automatic. You have to open it manually to go inside."

Still trying to figure out how to graciously refuse such trappings, she opened the door and stepped into a type of fairy tale. She expected a layout exactly as she'd just seen next door, but its design was totally different, and decidedly feminine.

"Mom usually only provides the basic furnishings for

guest homes," Noah explained as he came up behind her. "She likes whoever stays to be able to make it their own."

"It's...big."

Damaris crossed the foyer to a wide hall that led to an open-concept area. Beyond it was a kitchen and dining area with a bar counter running between them. Large, bare windows let in tons of light, along with sweeping views of the land around them. The grass was a vibrant green even as snowcapped mountains loomed in the distance.

"Is that a lake?"

"Yes."

"Man-made?"

"Designed by my father, Adam and another trout-fishing enthusiast."

"It adds to the beauty of the landscape."

The glistening water, tinged blue by the sky along with the verdant greenery and white-capped mountains was a breathtaking site. Utah was beautiful but Damaris had to give it to the Breedloves. They'd taken their land and fashioned a bit of paradise.

But she couldn't live here. That point was made plain moments later, as the tour continued.

"This is the master," Noah said, rolling into a suite the size of a small apartment. It was on the back side of the home, offering that glorious view of lakes and mountains.

"Go on in, take a look. If you're anything like the women in my family, you'll really love the closet. It's huge."

Damaris stepped into a sitting area separated from the actual bedroom by a half-wall bookshelf. There was a fireplace! In her bedroom! Leaving would be harder than Damaris first thought. Perhaps she was being silly to make such a big deal of living next door to Noah. Even though being alone in the home of a man who was not a relative, a man whose handsomeness awoke parts of her she didn't know were sleeping, was not Layman appropriate.

He's your patient. Get a grip! Her inner voice spoke with authority and gave her the courage to continue the tour, which included a guest bedroom, hall bath, the magnificent kitchen with everything stocked as Victoria had said and an outdoor sitting area that was enclosed and private.

They returned to the hallway. Noah pressed a hidden button. A portion of the wall lowered to reveal an electronic panel that worked everything from lighting to sound. He explained the intercom, video and security systems and then nodded toward a tray in the foyer that held a set of keys.

"A car for your use is in the garage. There's a walkway between our homes, through the garage, so that during inclement weather or when it's a million degrees you won't have to go outside."

He stopped, looked around. "I guess that's it."

"Thank you for showing me around. It's a beautiful home."

"If you need anything, just, um, hit me up on the intercom."

"Okay."

Noah made no move to leave. "Would you like to have a drink or something? I'd like to learn a little more about your role on the team."

"Sure."

Yes, let's talk professional. The more their conversations stayed focused on business the easier it would be for Damaris to remember why she was here, the only reason.

"Shall we see how well that kitchen is stocked?"

"Okay." Silly, but the simple statement made her nervous. She and Noah in her temporary home felt, well, too homey. In looking at him it struck her that this was the first time except for Matthew, or work, she'd ever been alone with a man who wasn't family.

"It's your place," Noah said, motioning for Damaris to go ahead of him. "After you."

They entered the kitchen. Damaris opened a panel of the double-door refrigerator that had been stocked with organic canned drinks. Next to it, a counter boasted a Keurig machine, and a wooden box holding a variety of coffees and teas.

"What would you like?"

Before the sentence was finished, Damaris realized the double entendre she'd thrown out. "To drink," she added.

Noah smiled, confirming that he'd totally caught it. "Whatever you're having."

She pulled two colas from the fridge and glasses from the cabinet. She filled them with ice, poured the drinks and began walking toward a patio door.

"It's not that cold and I noticed a firepit. Let's sit outside."

The seating area held a table and two chairs, the perfect height for Noah.

"I can't believe I'm here," she said, leaning against the chair's back. "How are you, Noah…really?"

"I'm okay."

Those eyes again, black, piercing, caused Damaris's stomach to flip-flop and made her mouth go dry. She took a long drink of cola, appreciating the burn as it went down her throat.

"This land, your home is beautiful. Everything here is like something you see in movies."

"It went up as fast as some do on a set. This place wasn't here two weeks ago."

"Your mother told me about the superfast build. I would have thought that impossible."

"Almost anything becomes possible when you stack the coins high enough. Dad and my brothers got together with a leading West Coast construction company who hired additional crew and had this built so I could get around in a wheelchair and…have help nearby."

"It's hard to believe that all of this was just built. The decor, furniture, everything seems cozy, so right for the room, as if lived in for a while. And outside, the lawn, all of the landscaping is impeccable."

Noah sipped his soda and surveyed the land. "My mom's vision, mostly, along with incredible architectural, interior design and landscaping teams. Not much happens beyond the gate without being put past her first." He sipped his cola and looked around. "Thanks for that, though. Nice to appreciate the land through a newcomer's eyes."

"Is she a part of the neighborhood association?" Damaris was eager to learn about the other families who lived here.

Noah frowned. "Huh?"

"We passed several homes before reaching the duplex. Do all of the owners participate in what decisions are made?"

"No, my mom pretty much runs things." He paused, smiling. "It's all Breedlove property, Damaris. The homes you passed belong to family or are guesthouses. The ranch is Adam's. He breeds that delicious beef you ate."

"Your brother is a rancher? He doesn't work in the family business?"

"All of us brothers work in the business. The ranch is a side hustle."

One that, according to Wendy's research, had made several million dollars last year. Damaris couldn't imagine making that much money per year working one job full-time, even two. Noah continued to watch her intently, making Damaris realize she'd stopped talking. Casual conversation was hard. The guy did things to her insides and made her want to squirm. She returned to the safe topics of medicine and healing, hoping to break the spell.

"I'm surprised at how quickly your facial injuries are healing. You can hardly see the cut on your forehead."

"Yeah, Ryan and a friend at the spa brought around their miracle potions. Looks like they're working."

"I look forward to visiting her practice one day. It includes a spa, as well?"

"The spa is part of our hotel."

"Oh."

Again, conversation faltered. She glanced at Noah from beneath her lashes, watched his fingers beat a silent rhythm on the arm of his wheelchair before finishing his drink. He was tense, too. After another few seconds of silence, they both spoke at once.

"I should really—"

"You probably want to—"

"Go ahead," Noah said.

"I was thinking to call my family and let them know I arrived safely."

"That's a good idea." Noah headed across the shared patio to his sliding glass doors. "No worries. I'll see you later."

"I'll come over to do a quick checkup—temperature, blood pressure, stuff like that."

"Only if you think it's necessary. Otherwise, it's okay if you take the rest of the day and get settled. I think I'll live until tomorrow."

"Okay, thanks, Noah. Verbal feuds aside, I look forward to helping in your healing journey."

His gaze intensified in an unreadable expression. "Me, too, Dee. Me, too."

Eleven

"There's a meeting at corporate tomorrow," was Nick's greeting the next morning after Noah opened the door. "You need to be there. This house is cool, so much so that I'm thinking about using that construction firm when I get ready to build. But you can't hide out forever."

"Who says I'm hiding?" Noah spat over his shoulder, wheeling himself through the living area and onto the patio beyond it.

"I'm saying it, bro." He followed Noah outside. "Not that I'm trying to be insensitive."

"Yes, you are. Dee would probably applaud the comment. I probably need a good kick to get off my pity pot."

"She's the more informal Dee now, huh? How's the pretty nurse working out?"

"Pretty well."

"Mom seems to like her."

"Mom likes every potential daughter-in-law."

"True that. From what I've seen so far, you could do much worse."

"Definitely couldn't do any better, not now. I can't imagine any woman in our circles wanting to spend their life pushing a chair around."

Noah's eyes narrowed. "Sounds like you need to expand your imagination. You're a good man, Twin, same as you've always been. Legs didn't make you and they will not break you."

"Easy for you to say. You're standing on yours."

Nick sighed as he sat on a patio chair. "I felt you that day, when it happened. It was late night in Africa. Chris and I had just left from having dinner with our hosts and were being driven home. We were riding along and something hit me. Bam! Like I'd been punched. Out of the blue. Ask Chris. He saw it and thought I was playing around. I wasn't. When we got the news about you a short time later, it wasn't a total surprise."

Nick stroked his chin as he looked over the land. "I hate what happened to you, man. It kills me, for real. I can't imagine you spending the rest of your life like this, so the only thing I can think of to do is encourage you to get better, to force life back to the way it was. I know it's only been three weeks and you're working hard to recover physically. It's your focus. I get that. I just know how much you love the business, how much that world is your normal. Makes your blood flood and your brain tick, just like me. I'm also a bit familiar with your type A personality and am not used to seeing someone else run your show."

His twin was right. When Noah returned to Las Vegas, he hadn't wanted to see anyone. He'd been in the news and knew everyone was wondering what exactly had happened. That his peers were curious as to the severity of his injuries. He couldn't stay hidden forever. He just hated the thought of being viewed by the public as that guy in the chair and pitied because of it. The thought of being labeled disabled was something he was loath to admit bothered him. But it did.

"You know what, bro? I'm an asshole, okay? Don't worry about showing up tomorrow. We'll video-conference you in if we need to. Just focus on getting better."

"Don't do that."

"What?"

"Start coddling me. Right now I need the asshole who cuts me no slack. Got it?" Noah held out his hand for a fist bump.

Nick leaned over with an outstretched fist. "Got it."

"Now, what's going on that I don't know about?"

Nick hopped up from the chair, walked over to a fridge in the outdoor kitchen and pulled out a bottle of beer. He held it up to Noah, who shook his head.

He returned to his seat and unscrewed the cap. "Dad didn't want me to say anything, at least not yet."

"About what?"

"The extent of your injuries is about to be made public."

"What? How?"

"Someone leaked the story to a major publication. We don't know who and Sandy won't name his source."

"Sandy is breaking the story?"

Sandy Lebowitz was a business reporter and longtime associate of the Breedloves. He'd done articles on them and the CANN organization for more than a decade.

"If he doesn't, someone else will. At least he had the decency to call the office, tell us what he had and give us, you specifically, a heads-up."

Noah spat out an expletive.

"I know. It sucks. But given how many people it took to get you here and the money a story like this could net, it was bound to happen."

A thought caused Noah's heart to almost stop beating. "Do you think it was Dee?"

"The nurse?"

"No, the groundskeeper."

"Whoa! Where'd that come from?"

"From the list of possible suspects."

Nick shook his head. "She doesn't seem like the kind of person to do something like that."

"I didn't think she was someone who'd take a job behind my back, either, but she did."

Noah could tell he'd shocked his brother. "You didn't hire her? Mom hired her without your input?"

"Yes and no. While at Manning Valley Medical she'd bring her up, asked me if I was satisfied with the level of care she provided."

"Are you?"

"Yes, but… I don't know. I guess that since she's a member of the conservative Church of Laymen, I'm just surprised she took the job. Unless…"

Nick leaned forward. "Unless what?"

"Unless she had an ulterior motive for coming here."

"What kind of motive? Money? Fame? She's a nurse, dude, and while I wasn't around her all that much at the hospital, I'm a pretty good judge of character and she didn't give off a gamer kind of vibe."

Noah wasn't listening. He was already halfway to the

patio door. Once inside, he went straight to his phone and tapped the face.

"Mom, I need to see Dee's résumé." He paused, frowned. "I don't have time to explain right now. Can you email it to me ASAP? I need to check something out, that's all."

He disconnected the call, turned and took in Nick's questioning gaze. "The Church of Laymen is the only reason the hotel bill is stalled in council. My paralysis becoming public could call my very competence into question and make it easier for those still deciding to be swayed back to the church's side. You feel me?"

"Not really. Dee didn't have to accept a position here to do that. She could have blown your cover while you were in Utah, had photographers snapping you on the stretcher, or inside the hospital. She could have tipped someone off when you were leaving so you'd be snapped in the chair. If she was the one who leaked what happened to the press, I think coming here and sleeping mere yards away from the person wronged is the last place she'd want to be."

Noah eased back against his chair. "You're probably right."

His phone dinged. He tapped the mail icon, downloaded the file Victoria had sent and opened it up. At the top of the one-page document in bold letters, all caps, was her full name: Damaris Glen.

One glance and Noah's hackles were raised. "No, can't be," he whispered. He did a quick internet search and confirmed the impossible. A major opponent to the bill, Franklin Glen, and Damaris Glen were not just related. Damaris was his daughter.

He went into his office and retrieved the tablet he'd placed there. "She's up to something."

"You're still talking about Dee?" By the tone of Nick's voice, he was clearly confused.

Noah's fingers flew over the touch keyboard. He used his forefinger to scroll down several pages until he found the information he wanted. "'Franklin Glen, Associate Pastor/Business Development, Church of Laymen.'"

"Okay." Said as a question, or statement, or both.

"She's his daughter, Twin," Noah said, fuming. "Damaris is the daughter of my toughest opponent, the guy fighting the hardest to keep gambling out of Utah and the casino bill from going through!"

"One more time. What could she gain from coming here to work for you?"

"I don't know," Noah said, heading toward the front door. "But she's good at keeping secrets, I know that. She accepted the job from Mom behind my back. Discussed gambling and Project Salt Lake City without once mentioning her father!" The more Noah remembered, the angrier he got. "So I don't know what's going on in that head of hers. But I sure as hell am going to find out!"

"Twin!" Nick hurried to catch up with his fast-rolling brother. He grabbed the handgrip just as Noah neared the door. "I understand you wanting clarification and more information. But go over there like the brother I know, the one that's too cool for school. There might be a logical explanation to whatever you're supposing. You don't want to offend the very person who's upended her life and relocated here to help you."

Noah took a breath. "You're right. Thanks, bro."

"The last time you got this heated over a woman, y'all were dating."

"Don't go there." Thinking about his corporate-ladder-climbing ex was the last thing Noah needed.

"I won't but you might. Damaris is fine."

He opened the door. Noah stuck up his middle finger as he went toward Dee's house. He could hear Nick's laughter as he reached the door and pressed the bell. Nick pulled out of Noah's drive and gave a honk as he drove away. Noah waved, and waited. Two minutes, longer. He rang the bell again.

Is she trying to avoid me? Does she have a feeling that her cover is already blown and she's coming up with a story?

Too cool for school began to feel like heat in the street as five minutes later, he was still on the other side of the door. He rang the bell a third time, then opened the screen, about to bang on the wooden interior door when it jerked open.

"Noah! What is it? Is there something wrong?"

At that moment all kinds of wrong happened, starting with the thoughts that ran through Noah's mind as he took in Damaris's freshly showered appearance. Her hair wrapped in a towel. A short silk robe hastily tied. Bare feet with toenails painted a lickable shade of coral pink. His eyes took a slow crawl from her feet to her face, one that eyed him questionably even as a blush dusted her neck and crept up her chin, making her even more attractive than seconds before.

"That's what I came to find out!" He took a breath and added more softly, "I'm sorry. I should have used the intercom."

"Why didn't you? What's the matter? Are you experiencing some type of physical discomfort?"

But for the fact that he couldn't feel below the waist, Noah was sure he'd be in the stiffest kinds of pain.

"How I feel physically has nothing to do with why I'm upset. We need to talk."

"I can dress and be over to your house in ten minutes."

"This can't wait," Noah countered, working to keep his anger in check. "We need to talk now."

She eyed him for a moment. "Okay, come in."

He entered the house, feeling justified though a bit embarrassed at how he'd almost been ready to beat down her door. How he acted around her wasn't like him. Damaris stirred something in him, a simmering fire. Crazy thing was, Noah wasn't sure he wanted it to be put out.

"Give me a moment," she said when they entered the living room. She left Noah alone with a chance to gather his thoughts, returning moments later with skinny jeans beneath the now properly tied robe, still-damp hair in a high ponytail, and feet bare.

She sat on the couch and pulled her legs beneath her. "Okay, what do we need to talk about?"

"Your father, Franklin Glen."

She'd almost contained any reaction, but Noah was an expert at people reading. He'd noted the slight widening of the eyes and stiffening neck.

"What about him?"

"Why didn't you tell me?"

"That he was my father? You didn't ask."

"So you lied by omission?" Noah asked.

"I didn't lie at all," Damaris replied curtly. "And I resent you insinuating that I did."

"You didn't lie and didn't come clean, either. All of the discussions about gambling in Utah, the Church of Laymen being the only reason the bill hasn't passed, and the thought to mention your dad's intrinsic involvement never came to mind?"

"It did, but obviously I decided against it. His position on gambling has nothing to do with my work as your nurse and my assisting the medical team. Keeping those two worlds separate seemed sensible then and, given your reaction, an appropriate decision."

Noah watched as Damaris leaned against the couch, the flash of anger gone from her eyes. She'd sounded sincere. Noah almost believed her, *almost* being the operative word.

"Are you sure there isn't more to the story? Given your unexpected arrival and the plans with my mother of which I was unaware, I think my question is *appropriate*." He repeated with emphasis the word she'd used to describe her decision. Her crossed arms signaled it irked her, as he knew it would.

"What exactly are you asking?"

"Are you here on his behalf?" Noah asked just as directly, believing a straightforward conversation was the best one to have.

What happened next was totally unexpected. Damaris cracked up. Not a polite chuckle, or a sexy giggle meant to tickle his senses. A full-out, head-thrown-back, gut-busting guffaw.

"You're kidding, right?" she finally asked.

"You know how hard we worked to keep the severity of my accident private, right?"

Damaris sobered a bit. "Yes."

"Well, someone leaked it to a major publication. The story is going to run next week."

"Oh, no. I'm sorry, Noah. Wait." The humorous gleam

in her eye disappeared. "You think I had something to do with that?"

"News of my…situation…could negatively impact Project Salt Lake."

"And you think I would disregard the hospital's privacy policy, ignore my own integrity and expose my patient's medical condition to somehow help my dad?"

"Business is a dirty game—"

"I'm not in business. I'm in health care. And I take strong exception to the implication of what you're asking. If I was going to expose you, why would I accept Victoria's offer? I was the second medical to see you after the EMTs, had full access to your records from the day you fell and ample opportunity to bring out the paparazzi or whoever covers people in the public eye. No, Noah. I haven't and would never talk to anyone outside the hospital about any of my patients, under any condition. Understand?"

He'd been properly chastised and damn if she didn't look delicious while doing it, especially since in her hand-gesturing, her robe had loosened to provide him the merest of glimpses to the fullness of a lovely breast. She followed his eyes and pulled the fabric together.

"Sorry, natural reaction." Noah looked away. "I admit to coming over with the preconceived notion that your father's position against our building a casino in your state may have something to do with you accepting this job."

Damaris's eyes slid from him to an arrangement of exotic flowers on a table across the room, then above them to the large living room window and the world beyond it. The look on her face combined with her silence made Noah feel foolish. Nick was right. Damaris wasn't the conniving type. Noah wasn't normally one to go off half-cocked. Then again, nothing in his life had been normal since he fell off a mountain.

"Why didn't you tell me that Franklin Glen was your father?"

"As I said before, you didn't ask. The names of my parents never came up in my conversations with Victoria and listing them on my résumé never crossed my mind. I assume you met him at one of the council meetings?"

"Assume? Given he's the church's primary representative at those meetings and acts on their behalf, you were probably sure of it."

"He doesn't discuss the church's business with me, but I felt there was a chance that you two had met. Dad is practical, pragmatic and honest. Everything he's seen about the impact of gambling has gone into his staunch opposition to your casino. Information I shared openly, by the way, while still in Utah. What made you think CANN could achieve what no one else has done? Legalized gambling in any and every form has been proposed and promoted over and again. No matter the package, each time it has tried and failed."

"No other method would bring as many jobs to the city as our casino hotel. It would attract tourists, who would then spend money at other businesses. There's a reason why your church is in the minority. A strong enough force to slow the progress, for sure, but not enough to stop it."

"If a better economy is your goal, why not do everything you've planned except without a casino? There would still be jobs and a reason to visit. Your hotels are known all over the world."

"Because without a casino, it wouldn't be CANN."

Damaris gave his comment some thought. "Let me give you some advice that you didn't ask for. There's no way a bill to build a casino in Salt Lake will ever pass. A large majority of its residents belong to the church. That said, and for the record, I'm not here for my father. I'm here for you, as your nurse and caretaker. The only fight I'm waging is one where you will walk again."

Undoubtedly, she meant those words. It showed in her eyes. His mother was almost always right. This time was no exception. Damaris was a great addition to the team.

"I believe you." He held out his hand. "Truce?"

She made a face and moved her hand farther away. "I don't know," she said, her voice coated with mock doubt.

The unexpected reaction made him laugh. "Come on, don't be like that."

She slowly stretched out her arm and placed her hand in his. Their eyes locked and held as she softly replied, "Truce."

He meant to release her hand, but the next thing he knew he'd pulled it to his lips and kissed it.

"Thank you."

"You're welcome."

So soft, Noah thought as, not wanting to let go, he turned over her hand. He resisted the urge to trace her lifeline with his tongue and instead used his finger.

"What are you doing?" she whispered, gently pulling back her hand.

It was a question to which Noah had no answer. He shrugged.

"I'm glad we cleared the air," she said.

"Me, too," Noah said, although to him the air was heavier than it had ever been, filled with unspoken words, hidden desire and the allure of something impossible, and off-limits.

When Noah left a short time later, the stormy encounter

had given way to calm waves of understanding. Damaris didn't know it but their talk had also given Noah a new dose of determination. To say that something could never be done made him all the more resolved to do it. Unwittingly, she'd given him something else. The first inklings of another possibility for a way to make it happen.

That idea, however, would have to wait. The most pressing issue was to get ahead of the story that would break in a few days. A meeting was hastily called involving Nicholas, Noah, the brothers, the company publicist and key staff members from CANN. Later that night, Noah posted a video on the company website, which was later sent to the major news networks and business publications. They couldn't keep the extent of Noah's injuries a secret. But they could somewhat control the narrative.

The shot was filmed in Noah's home office, a masterfully blended design of casual and contemporary. He sat behind one of his favorite furniture pieces, an antique mahogany desk rumored to have been owned by one of the state's founders. His stylist had suggested a business casual look and paired a tailed black suit coat with a pinstriped shirt and no tie. His hair was freshly cut. Though the suggestion was made to camouflage it with makeup, Noah decided not to hide the scar on his forehead. It gave him a roguish air. The camera crew set up a teleprompter and after several revisions and run-throughs, Noah delivered the message that he hoped would limit any potential damage to his prospective business deals once the news of his paralysis was out.

"Good evening. I'm Noah Breedlove with CANN International. Several weeks ago, as was reported on many news outlets, I was involved in a serious skiing accident on Daredevil Mountain near Manning Valley, Utah. What was not reported at that time was the extent of my injuries. Fractures occurred along my spinal cord that have rendered me temporarily paralyzed in my lower extremities. A team of world-leading specialists believes that I can and will make a full recovery. I'd hoped to already be walking, which is why I chose not to share this before. I disclose the challenge at this time not only because of the inevitable leak that is forthcoming but also as an otherwise healthy young man, a corporate executive who can put a somewhat public face on a disability that is experienced by thousands of people in this country and all over the world. I have a new appreciation for the brave men and women who experience what I have and still have the courage, strength and determination to live full lives, who do so whether they recover fully or not. My legs are temporarily out of commission, but my mind is still very much intact. I'll continue to kick butt, take names and make deals. To all of the CANN family and the customers we serve, thank you for your support."

Onscreen he came across as strong yet caring, successfully navigating the unexpected circumstances of his life. Inside he'd been a bundle of nerves. His mother assured him it didn't show.

"You were marvelous, honey. I'm so proud of you."

His dad, Nicholas, and all of his brothers praised him, as well. But it wasn't until the next morning when Damaris arrived to take his vitals and deliver his morning medications that Noah truly felt what he'd recorded had truly delivered.

"I watched your announcement," she said, pausing from her work to look at him directly. "I was moved to hear you share your heart, and relate to others, most without your resources, who are battling this same challenge. Noah, you'll never know how many people you helped."

"Let's just hope that my words prove true, your prayers work and my paralysis is indeed temporary."

"Either way, I think what you said was pretty amazing."

Noah hadn't realized how much Damaris's opinion about his taping mattered. But it did.

Twelve

That day after Noah left her house, Damaris didn't sleep much. She lay awake reexamining all of the choices and events that lined up to bring her here to work as Noah's nurse. She thought about the kiss, Noah's lips on her skin. As a woman, not a nurse. She allowed in memories that hadn't been revisited since Matt died. Too painful. Once shameful. The closest intimacy she'd experienced with a man because, until married, doing so was against the rules. The thing was, Damaris finally acknowledged, at least to herself, that she didn't agree with that rule, and many of the others she'd been taught as truth. But what was she going to do about it?

The woman she was becoming was a different person from the little girl her parents raised. Admitting that to herself was one thing but what did that mean? To go against the church was to go against her family. To leave one meant being shunned from the other. Were Damaris's beliefs strong enough to withstand those consequences? Even if the impossible happened and Noah's playful flirting developed into something more, if they actually began dating and developed feelings for each other. Would the Breedlove family and their love be enough? Could she ever gain enough to cover the loss of her family?

Last night, she'd seen a different side of Noah. She'd gotten a peek inside the heart of the man she nursed and had seen the sincerity and compassion just beneath his steely facade. Her father had labeled the Breedloves evil because of their business. Yet so far, she'd seen a kind, hardworking, close-knit clan that, ironically, in some ways resembled her own. Were they truly responsible if an adult came into their establishment and chose to gamble? How much of her viewpoint had been shaped by the church and her father? For the next couple days, while adjusting to her new environment and schedule, she pushed the matter aside. But she couldn't keep putting it off. She had to speak with her dad. There was no way she'd let him be blindsided with the news about Noah, then put two and two together and figure out that he was her new boss.

She waited until Thursday evening, just past dinner, when she knew her parents would be in the study enjoying a cup of tea. Her mother would be reading or working a crossword puzzle while Franklin enjoyed his one vice, a hand-rolled cigar. She reached for her own cup of chamomile as the call connected. Bethany picked up on the second ring.

"Hello, honey."

"Hi, Mom."

"How's it going, Dee? Ready to quit the job and come home yet?"

Damaris smiled. "No, Mom. It's going well. There is something I need to discuss, though. Is Dad with you?"

"He's right here."

"Can you put me on speaker?"

"Sure."

Damaris heard mumbling as Bethany covered the receiver to speak to Franklin and then muted background noises when she hit the button.

"Okay, Dee. Dad's right here."

"Hi, Dad."

"Damaris."

He was still upset with her decision. *No bueno.* It had been made, however, and there were new developments. Just because something was unpleasant didn't mean it could go undone.

"As you know, I don't usually share much of my work with you guys. The whole doctor/patient privilege, hospital confidentiality and all that. However, Dad, I recently learned that you know my patient, and that his already public profile is about to get more exposure."

"As long as you're not working for anyone who promotes gambling, there won't be a problem."

"My patient is Noah Breedlove."

"You will end that job tonight." Franklin's response was immediate and definite, made after the slightest pause. The call was going worse than Damaris thought it would, and she'd thought it would go really badly.

"That's not possible, Dad."

"Don't you sit there and tell me what you can't do. I will not have my daughter working for the devil and those Breedloves are his next of kin."

"Franklin," she heard her mother murmur in the soft tone that seemed to always soothe him. "Perhaps we can at least hear her out."

Damaris gave a succinct recap of what happened with Noah, from the time he was brought into Manning Valley's emergency trauma center until Victoria asked her to relocate and become his personal nurse.

"I went into nursing because I felt it was my calling," she finished. "Victoria told me that she needed my help, specifically, at a very dark time for their family. If I can bring in a sliver of hope, a ray of light, I felt it my duty to help her."

"I appreciate your passion, honey," Franklin said, from an obviously calmer state. "I really do. But there are plenty of local nurses with your same qualifications."

"Technically, yes, Dad. But she didn't ask them to come work for her. She asked me. I signed a six-month contract that is nonnegotiable. Noah's mother put in this special clause because the world as her son knew it was upended. She wanted a team that could provide consistency in what we all know is a very difficult time of rehabilitation. I felt I could do that and agreed to commit. I have to honor my word."

"If that family thinks they are going to use an employment contract to sway my mind on their casino operation by having my daughter become a part of it they can think again. They're using you, Damaris. Don't let a slippery serpent's tongue lead you astray."

Damaris chuckled. "You and Noah may have more in common than you realize, Dad. He made the same accusation about you, that somehow I'd taken the job to sabotage him."

Franklin persisted, undeterred. "What about the faith,

Damaris? How can you work for a family that promotes evil?"

Damaris hesitated before giving an answer. She'd asked a similar question of herself. "I am not working for the family, Dad, or have anything to do with the corporation that builds casino hotels. I was hired by Victoria as a caretaker for her son who was injured while skiing near where I work in Manning Valley. The only gamble is whether or not the team they've assembled and that I'm a part of can be successful in helping Noah heal."

"Not a gamble," Bethany said. "But a conviction, a belief. I understand your father's concerns but personally feel your heart is in the right place. I'll be praying for Noah, and for you."

"I don't like it," Franklin admitted. "I wish you'd spoken with your mom and me before signing the contract. I'm sure you didn't because you knew we wouldn't approve."

"I made the decision quickly, Dad, but not lightly, and understand your concerns. I've spent four years of college and time on the job around people who believe differently than we do. I can handle it."

"That's what you think. During those times, you were here in Utah, in close contact with your family and surrounded by faith. I'll call Pastor Sullivan," Franklin added. "To tell him you'll be in church on Sunday and joining their ministry while away from home."

Damaris didn't resist her father's antics, trying to control her life from four-hundred-plus miles away. She probably would have visited the church anyway, out of habit if nothing else. Truth be told, though, Damaris had started to question some of what the church taught as absolute truth. At school and work, she'd met amazing people who weren't Laymen, and knew of church members who were not saints. At some point she'd have to make her own choices. Noah had accused her of not doing enough of that.

The next night when Damaris's phone rang at 7:00 p.m., after working hours, she guessed it was either her parents, her friend Wendy or Pastor Sullivan's wife, Ruby, calling about her attending Sunday's service. Travis was on the clock with Noah. When she picked up her phone and saw the therapist's number, she felt instant alarm.

"Hi, Tee," she answered lightly, using the nickname he'd created, his Tee to her Dee. "Is everything okay?"

"Hope so. I need to ask a favor."

"About you leaving next week to handle a family matter? Noah already told me."

"Kind of, except needing to leave tomorrow instead."

"Really? Is something wrong?"

"Yes and no. My dad died last year—"

"I'm so sorry."

"Thank you. Anyway, Mom's downsizing and selling the home. We thought it would take a few weeks to close but the buyers are paying cash and need to move ASAP. I promised Mom I'd help her so…"

"No, of course. How can I help you?"

"I already have a guy from the rehab center covering my days off next week and someone to carry out his morning exercises. If you could execute Noah's nightly rubdown and get him ready for bed, I'd owe you big-time."

The request caught Damaris off guard, as did the image that Travis's bedtime request unexpectedly provoked, one not fit for Sunday services.

"I know it's on your days off and hate to ask. I tried

to find someone else from the rehab center but it's late and they didn't have an extra body to spare away from the clinic. I don't know if Noah would be open to doing the work at the center instead of private sessions. I guess if push came to shove…"

"Don't worry, I'll do it. What time?"

"His evening rubdown? In half an hour. I wasn't planning to fly out until next week and my flight leaves at 6:00 a.m."

"Got it."

"The table is in the rec room. Clothing changes are in the chest of drawers just inside his massive closet. Thanks for helping me out. I'll see you when I get back." Tee ended the call.

She had less than a half hour to put on her game face to spend time alone with a man, albeit a patient, who was not a family member. After a few minutes of indecision on what to wear, she donned the black jeans from earlier that day, pulled a favorite faded T-shirt out of a stack in her third drawer and slid her feet into a pair of sandals. She forced her mind to remain professional, recalling what she'd learned in an advanced class involving massages for musculoskeletal and spinal trauma. The one and only time she'd performed the task was during her senior year and a week's training at a nursing home. Her patient then was a spry, quick-witted seventy-nine-year-old. Something told Damaris that working on the body of the young, strapping Noah Breedlove would not be the same. At all.

Thirteen

"No worries, Travis," Noah said while rolling from the office to his bedroom. "Focus on your mom and the family. Everything here will work out."

He ended the call and continued inside the same massively designed walk-in closet that Damaris enjoyed. Other rooms of the duplex differed in design, but the bedrooms were identical. He went to a horizontal chest of drawers that spanned a short wall and pulled out a change of workout clothes, the baggy shorts and loose-fitting, sleeveless T-shirt he usually wore for Travis's nightly rubdown sessions. Tonight, though, it wouldn't be Travis. It would be Damaris. No big deal. She was his nurse, not his next hookup. Even so, he grabbed a pair of black linen drawstring designer duds and paired it with a black T-shirt that was tighter than the ones he wore with Travis. He removed his business shirt and undergarment and pulled the T-shirt over his head, then slung the shorts over his wheelchair arm and continued to the bathroom, where one look in the mirror reminded him that he hadn't shaved. Oh well. Too late for that. After washing his face and brushing his teeth, he picked up then put back a bottle of cologne on the counter. *Get it together, Noah. This isn't a date!* Somebody should have told his heart because as hard as it began beating a few minutes later when the doorbell rang, it surely felt that way.

He looked at the home security screen and pressed the intercom button. "It's open, Dee. Come on in."

Was it him or had he just added a bit of bass to his voice?

He headed down the hall to meet her. "Hi."

"Hi, Noah. I guess Travis told you I'd be covering for him."

"Yeah, I got off the phone with him not long ago."

"It has to be hard making a lifestyle change like that, for his mom I mean."

"I'd imagine," Noah said casually, while reading everything about Damaris like a bestselling novel. She was nervous, which surprised him given her profession.

"Are you okay with taking over for Travis? Because if not…"

"I'm a nurse, Noah. This is part of my job. Of course I'm okay with it."

Noah hid a smile at the physical change in her demeanor, the tight lips, squared shoulders and quiet resolve that she'd turned on and displayed in her answer.

She nodded at his slacks. "We need to get you changed out of those."

He lifted the shorts from the chair arm, turned around and threw over his shoulder, "Follow me."

They entered Noah's master suite. Damaris stopped just inside the doorway. "No way!" She continued inside and over to the contraption near Noah's bed. "You have a bod-riser! Those aren't on the market," she continued, eyeing both him and the device a bit incredulously. "I've seen a couple prototypes in industry mags but these aren't due out for at least another two years."

Noah stopped beside her. "I guess it depends on who you know."

"You'd have to know the inventor to get…" Realization dawned. "You know this person." Said with arms crossed, a side-eye and attitude, like *really, dude?*

Yes. Really.

"I don't but Dr. Woo does. Dr. Okoye, the man behind this marvelous wonder, is one of her colleagues."

He watched as Damaris inspected the machine with an almost reverent wonder. The Body Lift Assistant, nicknamed the body riser and shortened to bod-riser by the few lucky test users, was created by Nigerian Dr. Israel Okoye after a former college roommate was paralyzed in a diving accident. During a visit the friend complained of how mentally debilitating it was to be totally dependent on another, unable to do tasks as simple as using the restroom or dressing oneself. Dr. Okoye returned to Africa consumed with the desire to help his friend. Nine short months later, the first prototype for the bod-riser was presented at a medical conference in Switzerland. Dr. Woo saw it there and from that meeting came the connection that allowed Noah the opportunity for a modicum of autonomy.

"How has it worked out for you?" Damaris asked. "Are you able to handle certain tasks completely, yet?"

Noah shook his head. "I still need assistance getting from here—" he tapped the arm of his wheelchair "—to there." He nodded at the device. "After that, I'm good to go."

"Great! Let's get you transferred."

He saw what appeared to be a wave of relief come over her face, glad, Noah imagined, not to have to totally help him undress. He didn't know much about the Church of Laymen but couldn't imagine a church that banned gambling would be too allowing of flaunting one's nakedness with the opposite sex.

She positioned herself in front of him and with a strength that surprised Noah, lifted him out of the chair and into the riser.

"I'm impressed," he said. "You're stronger than you look."

"Thank you. It's all in the technique," she said, with a wink, her eyes taking in the surroundings. "Travis mentioned a recreation room?"

Noah frowned slightly. "He did?" A pause and then, "Oh, the rec room. For recovery, not recreation."

"Or maybe both since our goal is to re-create your ability to walk."

"I never looked at the word like that."

"Me, either, until now."

"Sounds totally appropriate. The re-creation room is on the other side of the great room, first door on the left. I don't think it was set up the day you arrived."

"I'll go check it out, then. See you there."

"Not so fast, lady. I can change into these shorts but haven't mastered jumping from here back into the chair."

"Oh. Sorry."

That delicious blush that he'd come to expect and appreciate began a slow crawl from the base of her neck.

"I'm messing with you. Step into the hallway if you'd like. It'll only take a minute."

It took seven minutes, a considerably shorter time than the average paraplegic could perform the same task, usually from a prone position. Noah did not take this fact lightly. He knew how fortunate he was to be a man of means, with money, connection and power. He wasn't one of those who professed that life was fair and the playing field was level. It wasn't. If that were the case, he'd be walking.

Damaris's professional yet friendly disposition, more relaxed than when she'd first entered, calmed Noah, too. She chatted casually while assisting him from the chair to the table, again using technically advanced wonders that made for an easier transition. He pushed a button that lowered the table. A lever reclined his chair and a harness allowed Damaris to handle the transfer without additional aid.

She placed a hand on Noah's leg. He knew because he saw her do it, yet a part of him swore he could feel her flesh—soft, warm—against him. It was phantom and fleeting, an impossible desire. He hadn't felt anything there since that day. He watched as she gripped portions of his legs, manually gauging the bone density and muscle tone much as Travis had once done. She wasn't Travis. Every inch of her reminded him of femininity, the strong type, like iron covered in velvet. She paused, pushing in an area of his lower thigh, her brow knit in concentration, her luscious lips pursed in thought. He imagined how it would feel to kiss them, then closed his eyes to blot out the image.

"You're in good shape," he heard her say dispassionately, her total focus seemingly on his lower extremities.

"It's good you were so healthy and worked out regularly. It makes recovery—"

"Re-creating," he corrected, opening his eyes once more.

"Yes, re-creating, much easier."

Something shifted between them while something else developed. It was a small shift, the merest of changes, but he saw it in Damaris's eyes when she smiled at him, and again, felt it in the touch that he couldn't really feel.

"How do you take your massages? Soft music and dim lighting or brightness and rock?"

"Rock? Ha! That must be a new type of therapy. Actually, neither. Travis just goes to work on me. We chat a bit. He asks questions. I answer them. Or vice versa. Otherwise, it's silent."

"Hmm. I wonder what your sister-in-law would think about that?"

"Ryan?"

"Yes, the holistic doctor."

"Good question."

"Glad you think so. I'll ask her. Meanwhile, I'd like to play something soft and relaxing. Some circles teach music as healing. I believe there is truth to that. Would you mind?"

"Not at all."

Noah instructed her on how to operate the panel in the main hallway that filtered music throughout the house and various rooms. He waited to hear something ethereal and heady such as the New Age music Ryan sometimes played in their home. Instead, the soft strains of a classical piano piece interrupted the silence, the reverberation of the lower chords quieting his soul. Without a word, Damaris returned to the room and began to work. He watched as she placed delicate yet strong fingers around his foot and began slow, firm circular motions from his foot to his shin and the area beneath the knee. Against the background of Debussy's "Clair de Lune," she stroked and kneaded his muscles, bones, flesh, spirit. She deftly pressed areas where, unbeknownst to Noah, knots had formed or tendons had tightened. He closed his eyes and allowed himself to be transported by the motion of the melody to another place, another time. He imagined his former buff body instead of the broken one, and that the massage being given was more sensual than standard therapeutic fare, albeit by a beautiful nurse. Riding the waves of relaxation, his mind wandered from thoughts of work and family to nothing at all. He felt good, more at peace than since the accident happened. Almost normal. In that moment, he didn't feel like a disabled patient. He felt like Noah Breedlove, and uttered a whispered gratitude to Damaris for the gift her hands had brought.

"What did you say?"

"I said…" His eyes fluttered open to find Damaris's head bent low to hear his whisper, those luscious lips mere inches from his own. Pure instinct took over. He raised his hand, placed it behind her neck and pulled her face closer.

"Thank you," he finished before raising his head to erase the short distance between them.

Her lips were even softer than he imagined, her touch, tentative. He expected her to pull back. Instead, something amazing happened. She increased the pressure, following him as he lowered his head back to the table. That simple act of acquiescence was like a starter gun at the Kentucky Derby, his passion like a Thoroughbred shooting out of the gate. His hand slid from the nape of her neck into her thick tresses at the same time his tongue pressed through her slightly parted lips. Their tongues met and danced—slowly swirling, tasting—in a leisurely, unhurried get-to-know. Just as he raised his other hand and placed it on her back, ready to gently press her lovely orbs against his chest for even more contact, she ended the kiss.

"Noah," she murmured. He felt her body straighten and then heard, "Oh."

It was a soft exclamation, a quick intake of breath, unnoticeable except for a lull in the music. He opened his eyes and met Damaris's unreadable gaze. She quickly broke contact and said nothing. But her skin was talking, a light blush across her entire face as she moved to the other side of his body. He was confused until his eyes fell and he glimpsed an erection—long, thick, undeniable—begging for attention. There was no room for embarrassment. Hot damn! Kissing Damaris made his dick work! The knowledge that what his grandpa Will called their third leg was in this small way functioning normally gave him hope that the other two would someday do the same.

He looked up to apologize but the lips still tingling with excitement and desire couldn't form the words. He wasn't sorry about anything that had happened. From Damaris's expression he didn't think she had any regrets, either.

Fourteen

The placid professional mask Damaris slipped into place hid a torrent of emotions. What the heck just happened? The kiss was something she'd later unpack. But why had a simple erection unnerved her? She wasn't unfamiliar with the male anatomy. She and Matthew had honored the church's mandate to not have intercourse until marriage but they hadn't exactly remained chaste. They'd explored each other's bodies. One time, Matt had even asked her to kiss him "there." She'd been filled with guilt afterward but in the moment, the act was exciting.

That her patient had gotten and seemed to be maintaining a healthy erection should not have surprised her. From advanced studies she knew this could occur and the reasons behind it. What bothered her were the less than professional feelings swirling around her heart. Why was she having such difficulty maintaining control of them?

Damaris prided herself on being able to remain compassionate yet emotionally detached from each patient she tended. Her mentor had assured it would benefit her long-term. Easier said than done. Even harder when her eyes traveled from his groin to his face to find him silently watching her. She willed the floor to open up and swallow her whole. When it didn't, she tried to mask her nervousness with a medical explanation.

"What you're experiencing is most likely a reflexogenic erection," she said calmly, as though talking about the weather. "The nerve endings controlling tumescence remain intact."

"Tumescence?"

"The, um, instrument becoming engorged."

"My penis?"

Was that a gleam Damaris detected in Noah's eye? She squared her shoulders and lifted her chin. She would not be intimidated. She was a professional. She could do this!

"Yes, Noah, your penis."

"What did you call it? A reflex…"

"Reflexogenic reaction."

"Not usually the way my body responds to a simple kiss."

Simple? Seriously? There was nothing simple about it. Damaris remained quiet and tried to control the oncoming blush but felt her face grow warm. Instead of feeling more in control by facing what had happened to her patient head-on, Damaris had gone from the frying pan into the fire. A part of her wanted to flee to the sanctity of her home. But Damaris wasn't a quitter. When she started a job, she finished it.

"If the nerves are working, why can't I feel it?"

"That is probably a conversation best had with Travis,

or one of the specialists." She began bending Noah's legs, performing the exercises Travis had detailed in the email he'd sent. "I'm sure that is only one of several questions you have regarding how the paralysis will affect your life in that area."

"I apologize if the question made you uncomfortable."

"Accepted."

Damaris wanted to say that she'd not been bothered at all but lying could lead to more questions. Instead of talking she focused on the exercises Travis had outlined. The massages, he'd explained via the messages, were designed to stimulate circulation and improve the patient's overall health. Blood was definitely circulating, Damaris thought, willing herself not to blush again.

For the next two days, Damaris was spared from performing Travis's duties by the therapist who worked at the rehab center and helped out on weekends. Neither brought up the kiss. Damaris tried to forget it happened. Still, something had shifted. Noah felt it, too. Their conversations were stilted, forced, almost too polite. At times she caught him looking at her and wondered if he did the same, then chided herself for fantasizing about dating him. His girlfriends were probably rich runway model types. It was silly to think someone like Noah would ever look romantically at someone like her. A conversation with her mother on Saturday night put the matter to rest.

"Dee, I'm worried about you," her mother, Bethany, said seconds after Damaris answered the phone. "I know you think you're strong enough to withstand that town's temptations but you've never been this far from home before, away from your family and church. Have you spoken with Pastor Sullivan, or Ruby, his wife?"

"No," Damaris said, remembering the unknown

caller she'd seen and ignored a couple times. She told her mother about them and added, "I probably should listen to my voice mail messages. I've been really busy."

"Not too busy to remember your faith, I hope. You must remember your place there, as an employee, nothing more."

"I know, Mom." Except her heart didn't.

"Be sure you do. Men like the one you work for might take liberties with a pretty girl like you but if and when he marries…it will be to someone whose values equal his. Clearly, yours do not. Correct?"

"Correct." The weight of her mother's truth caused Damaris to plop on her couch.

"Good. Your father spoke with the pastor and asked the family to look out for you. He has a daughter, Lori, who's close to your age. She's looking forward to meeting you at services tomorrow."

"I'll be there."

After Bethany's call, Damaris listened to her voice mails. Indeed, the pastor's daughter, Lori, had called. Damaris texted to let her know she'd received the message and would see her the following day. A restless night gave way to a rainy morning—a perfect match to Damaris's mood. She rolled out of bed determined to shake the doldrums, had just finished a quick breakfast and was headed to the shower when the phone rang. It was the house phone, not her cell, which meant one of two people were calling—Victoria, or her mom.

She quickly crossed the room. "Hello?"

"Good morning, Dee. It's Victoria."

"Good morning."

"I just realized I've been remiss in showing some good old Breedlove hospitality. You've not been invited to our legendary Sunday brunch and I'd be delighted for you to join us. Any time is fine but the meal officially gets underway at ten."

"Thank you for inviting me, Victoria, but I have other plans."

"Oh?"

"Yes. I've been invited to church by the relative of a member back home. I was headed for a shower when the phone rang."

"Okay. I hate that you won't be joining us but wanting to be in familiar surroundings is understandable. Have a wonderful Sunday, dear. I'd love for us to chat soon, perhaps lunch next week?"

"Of course."

"Great. I'll be in touch."

Damaris went to church. She met Lori, two years older, married to a man named Philip Bolton and expecting the couple's second child. She sat with them and Philip's best friend, "an upstanding Layman" named Steve. The sermon seemed tailor-made for Damaris, could have been written by her father. Pastor Sullivan admonished the congregation to avoid sustained interaction with outsiders, resist temptation and cling to the faith. When Lori invited her to dinner in their home later that week, Damaris accepted. It was the right thing to do. She sang familiar songs, recited familiar phrases and returned home feeling more conflicted than ever. She was still torn the next day as she headed to her final session with Noah before Travis returned, a swimming exercise like the one she'd briefly watched the week prior before administering a round of medication. That day she'd watched from a distance. Today she'd be in the pool.

Damaris reached the main house and followed the

drive to the infinity pool at the back of the home. Globed lighting outlined the pool against an inky black sky, dotted with a thousand stars. The shiver that ran down her back as she spotted Noah already in the pool had nothing to do with the chill in the air. Nick and his father, Nicholas, were seated at a nearby patio table, chatting as Noah lay on a floating device, with additional floaters around each biceps. They stood as she reached them and, after exchanging greetings, beat a hasty retreat.

Damaris tilted her head toward the retreating figures, made her voice light even though upon seeing Noah her heart beat wildly. "Was it something I said?"

"They were just keeping me company until you arrived."

"Are you ready to begin?"

"Sure."

Damaris slipped off her sandals and walked toward the pool steps.

"What are you doing?"

"Getting in the pool," she responded, well aware of why the question was asked. Not having packed a swimsuit for her time in Nevada was only one reason she'd planned to conduct the session wearing an extra large T-shirt over a sports bra and knee-length baggy shorts. Modesty was another. Fear of inciting further attraction or arousal, by either party, was a third.

"Where's your swimsuit?"

"Don't have one. Besides, the temperature is dropping and I'm cold-blooded by nature. My getting sick won't improve your health."

Noah used strong strokes to guide the float toward the pool's edge. "The pool's heated, Dee."

She dipped a foot in the water. The temperature was

perfect, no cover-up needed. She began descending the pool steps.

"You need a suit," Noah replied.

"It's one exercise for thirty minutes. I'll be fine."

"Not acceptable," he said as she waded through the water to reach him. "There's extra swimwear in the pool house, purchased specifically for unprepared guests. Go get changed."

Damaris eyed Noah's broad chest and rock-hard abs. Instead of joining him in swimwear, she wanted to give him an oversize T-shirt. This outsider was too much temptation. "This will do for now. Come on, let's get started."

"Street clothes are not allowed into the pool," he replied with a calm authority and an expression that conveyed the word *no* wasn't an option.

Damaris huffed but didn't argue. Clearly, Noah was used to having orders followed. She was his employee. How could she argue? Plus, she felt this was another test—Noah purposely seeing how she reacted when pushed out of her comfort zone. She was determined to prove to both him and herself that she could resist the unspoken yet growing attraction between them. Once inside the pool house, Damaris continued to a room that looked more like a boutique. She quickly spotted a conservative black one-piece with matching cover and in less than five minutes was heading back out the door. The image that greeted her once back outside stopped her short. Noah, resting on the floater. God help her but his body was gorgeous.

Back outside she quickly shimmied out of the cover-up and into the pool. Beginning the exercises were more for her than him. Total body stretches. Knee-to-chest pull-ups. Intensive core work. Noah's abs were like stone. Muscle retention resistance. Noah put 100 percent into the workout and looked amazing while doing it. Had Damaris completely flummoxed and confused. Utah was full of great-looking guys. Some of them went to her church. What was it about Noah that caused her insides to quiver and certain body parts to pebble and pulse? Seeing him now was not that different from every night when she massaged his shins, thighs and buttocks and applied the ointment Ryan made to prevent blisters and sores. She should be used to seeing his bronzed body by now. Only she wasn't. That was a problem. Crushing on a patient was so not cool.

They finished the last exercise thirty minutes later.

"I think we're good," Damaris said. "What do you think?"

"We're finished with my workout. What about yours?"

"Trust me, I'm fine." As long as she didn't look at the lips she longed to kiss again.

"What, you scared to lose to a guy with no legs?"

Damaris's eyes narrowed. "Don't do that to yourself."

"Let's line up." Noah eased himself along the pool's edge to the shallow side of the pool.

"You're serious?"

"You tell me to think positive, right? I believe I can beat you."

Damaris was dubious but appreciated his moxie. "Okay." She waded through the water to the side of the pool. "Ready, set, go!"

She waited a beat before pushing off from the wall. In that instant, Noah was several strokes ahead of her. Even without the use of his legs, he went faster than she thought he would. After pushing off the wall, she used powerful freestyle moves in an effort to catch up. About midway through, she got even with him and then started to pull ahead. She kept going, not wanting it said that she'd "let him win." She was just a foot or so from the wall, ready to touch and claim victory when...

Whoosh!

Damaris was pulled back and underwater by a powerful force. The move was unexpected and caught her off guard. She did a flip underwater and pushed off the swimming pool bottom to rise to the surface. In the process the band she had around her hair came undone. It took several seconds to catch her breath and remove a blanket of wet hair from her face. When she did, it was to find Noah balancing himself on the winning end of the pool, laughing his head off.

"You!"

"I won!"

"You cheated!"

"I didn't say how I'd finish first, only that I would."

Damaris swam over to where he was gloating. She reached him and with no warning, splashed water in his face. Taken aback, he coughed and sputtered before returning the favor. The water fight was on, each splash getting bigger and more forceful than the next. A drenched Damaris made a move to get away. With one hand gripping the lip of the pool, Noah caught her leg with the other. His strength surprised her. He pulled her to him, then quickly let go of her leg to grab her waist.

"Now who's fighting unfair?"

"Let me go!" Damaris squirmed, trying to break Noah's viselike grip.

"Promise not to splash me again."

"I promise nothing!"

"Then I can't let you go."

Damaris stopped squirming and looked Noah in the eye. In that instant the mood changed. Their close proximity, his hard frame and lean fingers gripping her waist, those hypnotic eyes, all hit her in an instant. One small move, and she could kiss his wet, smiling lips. She felt restraint slipping. "Let. Me. Go."

His eyes became darker, dropped down to her lips. "Say please."

She licked her lips. "Please."

"I like your freckles," he said, still holding her, his eyes shifting to her mouth. "Your lips, too. I want to kiss you again."

Damaris eyed his lips also—full, wet, experienced—and imagined hers pressed against them. Her head lowered of its own accord as control began slipping away. Just before their lips touched, her mother's words came to mind. *Men like the one you work for might take liberties with a pretty girl like you...* She placed a hand on his chest and pushed to get away. His hard muscles and wet skin made her fingers tingle. She felt conflicted with desire and forced away the feeling.

"We need to get you out of the water," she said in a voice more breathless than she would have liked.

"Are you sure?" Noah asked, his intense gaze searing her soul.

"Yes," she managed, on a shaky breath. *No!* her body cried.

"Isn't a—" he thought for a second, then continued "—reflexogenic reaction good physical therapy?"

"Physical therapy is over, Noah," she replied.

He released her. She felt the loss, keenly. Now they were headed to his house for his nightly rubdown before preparing him for bed. With her luck he'd probably get another erection. *Just great*, Damaris thought as she exited the pool and pulled on the cover-up. *That's. Just. Great.*

Fifteen

Both personally and professionally, Noah's decisiveness had always been an asset. If he wanted something, he fearlessly went after it. Until now. The injury changed everything. He was attracted to the pretty nurse who'd captivated him from the moment they'd first locked eyes, but the possibility of rejection haunted him. There were many questions that needed answering, starting with why Damaris had rushed out of the pool.

He waited until they'd reached his home and once there, he informed Damaris that tonight he wanted a simple rubdown in his bed instead of on the massage table.

"Why?" she'd asked, as he knew she would, which was why he had an answer.

"I'm tired. Plus, less work for you. Once done I can say good-night and roll over."

Damaris considered his answer. "Works for me."

After exchanging wet swim trunks for a pair of comfy drawstring pants, Damaris helped him into bed. For a moment, he watched her work, while trying to exercise mental control and not allow errant thoughts to wake his snake. Considering what he was getting ready to bring up, there were no guarantees. In fact, the very opposite could occur.

"I want to ask you something," he began. "As a woman, not my nurse."

A quick look and slight brow raise were Damaris's only reactions. She finished rubbing down one leg and shifted to the other.

"Back at the pool, why didn't you kiss me?"

Her hands stilled for the briefest of seconds, before the kneading resumed.

"You wanted to," he told her.

"I did," she answered.

He wasn't surprised at her honesty. "Then why didn't you?"

"You have to ask?" She spoke without looking away from her task.

"We kissed before."

"That was a mistake."

"Says who?"

"Propriety. What happened the other night was inappropriate, and unprofessional."

"What we're discussing is personal, isn't it?"

"Not for me."

"Because you're my nurse."

"That and also because it's how I was raised."

"You were taught to ignore your feelings?"

"I was taught to follow the rules," Damaris finally said.

"Whose rules?" Noah shot back. Her short, simple answers were irritating, as was the emotional shield she hid behind. Noah was convinced that a blazing heat smoldered beneath her cool, aloof exterior. He wanted to be the one who stoked it, brought her to the type of erotic rapture he was sure she'd never experienced before. He wished certain body parts were working that would allow him to claim her completely. But there were other ways in which he could satisfy her. Noah knew them all.

He changed tactics, deciding on a less combative approach. "Was I mistaken about what happened the other night, and was almost repeated in the pool? Do you not find me attractive?"

"I find you very attractive," she admitted.

"Then is it because of my injuries, because I'm in a chair."

"Of course not!"

"Then you'd date me?"

"No," she quickly replied. Then, "I don't know," in a softer, less sure tone.

Noah shrugged. "I can't imagine the women I know dating a disabled guy."

Finished with the rubdown, Damaris washed her hands before reaching for a digital body reader. "What does your girlfriend think about it?"

"Is that your way of asking if I have one?"

"Never mind. That question wasn't professional, either. Quiet while I take your blood pressure."

Noah did as she instructed, watching her intently. He appreciated the command she exhibited in going about her duties, taking care of him, helping him get better. Being only twenty-five he'd never given serious consideration to what he'd want in a long-term relationship, or a marriage. He decided that some of the traits he saw in Damaris should be on the list.

"I don't have a girlfriend," he offered, when she was done. "Were you seeing anyone back home?"

"No," Damaris said after a pause.

"Were you dating?"

She shook her head.

"Why not? You're a beautiful girl."

"I was engaged. My fiancé was killed in a motorcycle accident. Placing all of my energy and focus into nursing helped me get past the loss."

"That had to have been difficult. I'm sorry."

"Thank you."

"Are you past it, the tragedy?"

"That's a good question," Damaris answered.

"How will you know?"

"I guess when my heart opens up to let someone new inside."

Their eyes met. He held the gaze. Damaris looked away. He wanted to kiss her again, longed to pull her into his arms and see if doing so produced another erection. He wanted to be able to feel that erection, to do what came naturally when such occurred. Instead he reached up and caressed her arm.

She stood abruptly, made a final notation on her tablet, then placed it in the tote she'd brought into the room. "I'm all done here. Is there anything I can get you before calling it a night?"

Plenty, Noah thought, but now was not the right time to ask. Instead he lowered the top portion of the bed to a fully reclined position and pulled up the cover.

"Sweet dreams, Damaris," he said.

"Good night, Noah."

It was a long night. Noah spent most of it trying to forget how good Damaris had felt during those few but precious seconds they play-fought in the pool. How softly yet firmly her hands massaged his immobile limbs. The way she avoided his eyes while doing her job. It was clear she'd been uncomfortable with the subject of dating, but she hadn't backed away. His disability would take him out of the running, for most women he knew anyway. But could someone like Damaris be interested, even if he never walked again? Would he be interested in someone like her, unworldly, conservative and sexually immature, if not for the chair? Did it matter, considering her religious stance against gambling when his family owned one of the largest casino operations in the world?

The next morning, Noah was up and out of the house an hour and a half before Travis was due to show up and drive him to the office. He dressed with minimal assistance, wheeled himself to the van and, ten minutes later, was headed to the main estate. Last night he'd sent a group text calling for a family business meeting to be held ASAP. Grappling with his feelings for Damaris and her father's direct opposition to them doing business in Salt Lake City had led him to an idea he felt could be total trash or pure genius. He needed his family's help to decide.

As he entered the home, greeted his mom and continued on to his father's study, he mulled over the plan, knew it could work, had to work. Noah knocked, then opened the door. His father was there, behind the desk, looking like the big baller shot caller even in a silk robe. Christian was there, too, enjoying one of the family chef Gabe's legendary cinnamon rolls. It didn't surprise him that Nick wasn't there yet but that he'd beat Adam to the meeting hadn't been expected. His rancher brother was usually up with the sun.

He walked in and gave a hug and handshake to the men in the room. "Where's Adam?"

"On the way," Nicholas said. "An overseas client called just as he was heading out the door."

"Problems?"

"No, thank goodness," Nicholas said, the relief clearly evident in his voice. The Breedloves had banded together to help Adam overcome a very challenging situation, one that could have cost him his ranching business, the family, even more. They did not want to ride that pony again.

Christopher reached for a napkin. "Where's your twin?"

The door opened. No knock. "Who's asking?" Nick strolled in and headed straight for the coffee, Adam two steps behind him.

"Who called this early-ass meeting," Nick mumbled, "and what's it about?"

"I did, bro," Noah replied. "Your second question will be answered shortly. Morning, Adam."

"Morning, family!" In direct opposition to Nick's appearance, Adam was showered and dressed in a tailored suit, his eyes bright as though he'd risen with the dawn.

Noah gave Adam a shoulder bump as he watched a disheveled Nick add three helpings of espresso to a caramel latte, then walk over to a leather recliner, plop down and lie back. No one had to ask how he'd spent his night. The only question was the one Adam asked.

"Who was she?"

"No time for that," Noah interjected. He pulled a folder from his briefcase and passed a one-page document to his brothers and dad. "After careful consideration, I'd like to make a few slight revisions to the Utah casino proposal."

"Like not building it in the first place, as was my suggestion?" Nicholas asked, without looking at the paper. "As it is, we've got about a half dozen investors ready to pull out."

"And another half who are unlikely to trust us again," Christian added.

"Thanks, bro, Dad, for your continued support."

Noah added a half smile and put up a hand to ward off further comment. He appreciated his dad's and brother's honest opinions. They removed any trace of nervousness and allowed him to get straight to the point.

"I'm more convinced than ever that ours should be the first gambling operation in the state of Utah."

"In Manning Valley?" Adam asked, looking up from the paper. "Besides those who run the Daredevil Ski Resort, do people live there?"

"Not many, which is why it's the perfect alternative to building in Salt Lake. Manning claims about ten thousand residents, with about a hundred thousand living in surrounding towns. Manning Valley Medical is the single biggest employer and, aside from ma-and-pa businesses, the only one. A CANN hotel would help grow the town, which officials want to do."

"That's not a minor revision," Nicholas said.

"It's a necessary one, Dad. The Church of Laymen's reach doesn't extend that far south. The town is struggling. It would be a win-win. The other revision will not only yield higher profit margins but get us past the religious argument against gambling in their state."

"Virtual machines." Noah pulled out another sheet of paper. "I've analyzed research and crunched the numbers." He looked at his siblings pointedly. "That's what I do, better than anybody."

A statement no one tried to dispute.

Instead, Nick asked, "How much of this has to do with the pushback from the church and your interest in one of its pretty members who just happens to be your private nurse?"

"It has everything to do with her."

The honest answer sat the twin straight up.

"Well, damn," Adam drawled.

Christian, too, looked surprised. But no one was more taken aback than Noah. He'd never admitted this truth to himself, let alone considered saying it out loud. But he had. Nothing to do but push forward, even more confident. In for a penny, in for a pound.

"While there are a growing number of politicians, law-makers and businessmen becoming more open to legal gambling in Utah, even in the face of staunch opposition, the church's pushback and amount of power wielded there was underestimated, especially in Salt Lake. The size of the city, its proximity to Provo and Park City, and the in-frastructure already in place made it the obvious choice. A conversation with Damaris, however, led to a broad-ening of my perspective and along with it the amount of available possibilities to get this done."

"Outside the CANN model, too," Christian said, look-ing up from the paper he held. "A virtual casino, bro?"

"Exactly, in Manning Valley, with customized lux-ury buses that pick customers up from the airport, and stop at other towns along the way. They'll be brought to a place that looks very similar to an actual casino ex-cept all of the gambling is actually done online, and the payouts, too."

"I don't like it," Nicholas said. "People go to a casino because they want to gamble. If they only want online games, they can play those from home."

"People go to a casino for the experience," Noah said. "Most slot players are already using digital screens."

"What about table games?" Christian asked. "I can't see gamblers getting too excited about virtual cards for poker and blackjack and rolling dice from a screen."

"I agree. Table games will happen in a different section of the casino, one where membership is required. This will be incorporated into our club rewards program and handled when the customer applies to get discounts and points.

"Technically, it is the exchange of money that defines gambling and is not allowed in Utah. By making ours a cashless casino, where players use cards containing money held in another state, that law is averted. The card will work as cash, usable wherever credit or debit cards are taken. Later this week, I've got a meeting with United States Capital, the largest bank in America and one we've used almost since this company's inception, to talk about how they can handle the financial component."

Nick, clearly intrigued, sat up in his chair. "But why Manning Valley instead of a town closer to Salt Lake?"

"As I explained, fewer Laymen," Noah answered. "Our research shows that residents there who belong to the church number less than fifty percent. Plus, it's a growing community eager to expand. The amount of jobs our project would create, along with the complementary businesses that could grow as a result, is very attractive to the city execs. Finally, we could buy twice the amount of land in Manning Valley for less than what we've budgeted for the state's capital."

"Son, I've been hesitant on this project from the beginning. But with this brilliant new concept, you're about to change my mind."

"That gives me hope, Dad. If I can convince the man who's mastered the hotel casino game and landed us at the top, maybe I can get those naysaying Laymen to play, too."

For the next hour Noah further laid out his vision for touch screen slots and bingo, horse race and sporting theaters and the elaborate financial system that would deliver winnings directly from a bank outside Utah to casino debit cards, with no direct cash exchange happening within the state. By the time he left his father's office, the family was on board. With their wind of support beneath his wings, Noah was unstoppable.

"Twin!"

Noah hadn't noticed Nick trailing behind him. "Hey, man."

"Let me catch a ride to the office."

Noah eyed him suspiciously. "Something wrong with the Lamborghini?"

"Not as cool as your tricked-out van," Nick replied.

"Get in. I'm going to swing around and pick up Travis. Not sure I'm ready for the freeway just yet."

Minutes later they were heading out of Breedlove. Nick kept up a running dialogue during the twenty-five-minute ride to the Strip. Noah was glad for his brother's company. It kept thoughts of the moment's significance at bay and with it, Noah's whirling emotions at being able to return to work at all. As the van turned into the entrance, he took in the familiar sight of the CANN Casino Hotel and Spa sign sparkling against the waterfall backdrop. He forced down the complaint that jumped to his throat when the physical therapist parked in a handicapped spot. Nick hopped out on the passenger side. Travis opened the side door and patiently waited as Noah maneuvered the chair onto the lift, then pushed the button, lowering himself to the ground. Travis reached back inside and retrieved his briefcase.

"Are you sure you don't want me to go in with you?" he asked, as he handed it over.

"We've got this," Nick answered, confident that together there wasn't anything the twins couldn't do.

Noah appreciated his therapist's concern. "We're taking the private elevator and won't encounter many people. Just be back to pick me up around seven tonight."

"That's almost nine hours," Travis protested. "It's your first day back, Noah. You might want to take it easy."

"That's what I've been doing for the past few weeks."

"The long day concerns me but you know your body. Just call if you need anything, or if you want me to come back earlier."

"He won't," Nick said, offering a fist to bump. "But thanks for looking out for my brother. You do a good job."

They headed down an outer hall leading from the parking lot to the interior. Nick's cell phone rang. Noah watched his brother listen to the caller, then glance at him.

"Um, sure. But can I meet you in a half hour or so? I want to get my brother settled—"

"Who is it?" Noah interrupted, and stopped moving.

"Hold on a minute." Nick muted the call. "It's Tiffany. She's here and wants to meet for breakfast."

"Go."

"I will as soon as—"

"You don't have to babysit me, bro."

"Doesn't matter."

"I know this building like the back of my hand, and I know how to wheel a chair. Plus, I know how Tiff has you wide-open right now so...go meet your girl."

"Are you sure?"

"Positive." Noah could tell his brother wasn't convinced. "I want back my independence."

"I can understand that. All right, bro. See you at the conference."

They entered the hotel. Noah watched his brother walk in the opposite direction, toward a set of public elevators that would land him in the south tower, closer to the hotel's boutiques and restaurants. He continued to the executive elevator and pressed his thumb against the scanner.

He took a breath, tried to relax muscles that were suddenly tense. It was his first time out of Breedlove, the first time he'd been without Damaris, Travis or a medical professional. Outside the estate, this was the first time he'd been alone in his chair. It was foreign, unsettling. He felt isolated and vulnerable but refused to give in to the fear. Everyone in the company had been very supportive. Noah began to relax.

The elevator arrived. So far, so good. Rolling into the car, he scanned his thumb for the floor available only to the top executives. The elevator doors opened to the gleaming CANN executive offices foyer and the smile on the receptionist's face lit up the room.

"Noah!" she cried, before jumping up, racing around the counter and offering a crushing hug. Smiles, tears and heartfelt greetings continued from there to his office and on to the boardroom, where he entered to a standing ovation and thunderous applause. Within seconds, all of Noah's trepidations about returning to the workplace fell away. Except for the fact that his chair now had wheels, it was just like any other day as a CANN executive. He allowed only a brief update on the article regarding his paralysis and the video produced as a result before taking control of the meeting and outlining the innovative new direction and location for the Utah casino, an idea spawned from his and Damaris's gambling debate. The pushback was expected, the voiced concerns valid. Noah listened. His counterarguments were sound. He went home exhausted yet more determined than ever to get his life back on track all the way around.

A ringing landline greeted Noah as he unlocked the front door and wheeled himself in. He reached for the one on a desk in the foyer and checked the ID.

"You must have seen the van," he said to his mother, placing the call on speaker.

"Good evening, son."

"Good evening. I'm fine. The day went great. Yes, dinner has been prepared. No, I'm not hurting. I have twenty minutes to eat and unwind before exercises with Mr. Relentless." Victoria's increased laughter as he continued answering the questions he assumed she'd called to ask made Noah smile. "Anything else?"

"Actually yes, dear. One, can you conduct your business from Denmark for the next couple weeks and two, does Dee have a passport?"

Sixteen

Damaris headed toward dinner with Lori Bolton, her husband, Philip, and their kids, with a growing sense of unease in the pit of her gut. How would the new Dee she'd just embraced interact with the old ideals she was sure to encounter around tonight's dinner table? She'd tried calling Wendy just to hear her thoughts out loud but her friend was doing a double shift and wouldn't be off until midnight. So here, just minutes away from a certain interrogation, Damaris grappled with a headful of clashing speculations on her own. When her phone rang and interrupted them, she was grateful.

"Hello?"

"Dee. Noah."

The mere sound of his voice made her squirm. She did her best to keep the excitement she felt out of her voice. "Hi, Noah. What's up?"

"Do you have a passport?"

Damaris frowned. "No, why?"

"Mom was wondering. Says she tried to reach you earlier, but it went to voice mail."

Only now did Damaris remember seeing Victoria's missed call. "I saw that and meant to call back but time got away. I'm having dinner with someone from the church but will call her afterward if it's not too late."

"I'll tell her."

"Why was she asking about a passport?" Damaris asked, exiting in Henderson, Nevada, as she followed GPS directions from a staid male voice with a British accent.

"Because the team wants to use treatments and products that won't clear customs because they don't have federal approval. They want to bring the patient to the potential cure instead of the other way around."

"They want you to fly to Scandinavia?"

"Yes, said I'd probably be over there a couple weeks. I'd want to maintain the already established regimen, of course, and bring you with me."

Damaris was too shocked to give a quick reply. She'd always wanted to travel out of the country but would never have guessed taking the job with Victoria would have been the way to do it. Would have never dreamed that first trip abroad could be with a man like Noah. An arrangement that the old Damaris wouldn't have considered at all but had the new Dee throbbing in unspoken places.

"Dee, you there?"

"Oh, yeah, sorry. I was just thinking, digesting that news. It sounds wonderful, but that you'd want me to come along is a surprise."

"Dr. Woo and the team thought it best. Travis will come over initially, as well."

"Oh." Adding that little tidbit made his reasons for asking crystal clear—business, not pleasure. Good. It would be okay for her body to fly in the clouds but she didn't need her head there, too.

"Tell me more about these treatments."

"I only got briefed by Mom, who says that while I was at work and unavailable she was on the phone with them for well over an hour. What they have is a new and largely untested form of treatment involving laser surgery on parts of my spine that were affected by the fall combined with these stimulators attached to various nerve points through fiber-optic braces."

"Robotics."

"I guess."

"Bionic legs!" Damaris's excitement grew as she reached Lori's neighborhood and followed the Brit's directions to a block of complementary homes covered in various shades of stucco and sporting red tile. She pulled into the two-car drive and parked behind a white Ford truck.

"Wow, Noah, that's fantastic! I remember reading something about this being developed during my junior year at college. The design was these sleek rubber sleeves that looked natural under clothes and are far less cumbersome than their steel counterparts. Did you see them?"

"I did."

"And you're not excited? It's a radical form of treatment that, once perfected, may revolutionize the industry and allow all paras and quads to walk. People like you, Noah, might walk again!"

"In theory, yes, but it's not definitively proved."

"That's what the testing is for, correct?"

"Yes. That's why they want me to fly to Denmark."

Damaris turned off the engine. "Why don't you sound excited?"

"I'm cautiously optimistic. But work is here, with major projects on the table. It's a critical time."

"Your health should be your main focus," Damaris said. She looked up to see Lori waving from the steps, a mini-me clutching her pant leg.

"Noah, I have to go. How do I get a passport?"

"We'll take care of all that. My assistant will send over the paperwork right away. Return it ASAP, later tonight if you can. This process usually takes anywhere from a few weeks to a couple months, but I have a contact in DC who can push the application through."

"Okay. I'll fill it out and return it tonight. Bye, Noah!"

Damaris exited the car with a big smile on her face. She hurried up the walk and hugged her host.

"Come on in," Lori said, eyeing her keenly. "Wow, someone looks happy."

"I am," Damaris gushed. She mussed the hair of the little girl beside her before walking through the door Lori held open. "I'm traveling out of the country...to Denmark!"

"What's over there?" By her tone Lori was clearly not as excited.

"Innovation," Damaris replied, in a tone more subdued. "Something smells good," she added, going for safer ground.

"Nothing fancy," Lori said. She led them into the dining room, where Philip sat chatting with another man. They stood when the ladies entered.

Damaris recognized the guy at once, Philip's best friend. She should have guessed their invite on Sunday wasn't just about dinner. The uneasy feeling from the drive over returned.

"Hello, Damaris," Philip said, his hand outstretched. She shook it as he spoke. "You remember my good Layman brother Steve. I hope you don't mind that we asked him to join us."

Would it have mattered, was her inward thought. Outwardly she smiled. "Hi, Steve."

He took her hand in both of his, eyes shining with open admiration. "Good evening, Damaris. It's wonderful to see you again."

She gently pulled her hand from his grasp and took a seat as Lori directed, working to hide her chagrin at being set up. Not even five minutes inside and Damaris already knew. It was going to be a long night. Small talk ensued as the first course, a simple salad, was served. Once church news and weather observations ran out, the conversation became all about Dee.

"I hear you're a nurse," Steve began, reaching for his glass of soda.

Damaris nodded.

"That's what brought you here?"

Another nod, around a bite of lasagna. The thought came to keep her mouth full and chew her way out of more detailed explanations, but one look at Steve and she knew that ploy had little chance of working. He was obviously smitten, the Boltons matchmaking. That this was a marriage mission couldn't have been more blatantly signaled if they'd put that message on a balloon tied to the back of her chair.

"Not at a hospital, though," Lori said.

"Your father tells us you're working for those billionaire Breedloves." Philip didn't try to hide his disgust. "I couldn't believe that as a Layman you'd accept their employ, or as his daughter, Glen would allow it."

Damaris took a moment to wipe her hands with a napkin, then enjoyed a sip of tea. She owed no one an explanation, yet briefly explained how she'd met the family and Victoria's request that she help Noah full-time.

"They are not Laymen," she concluded, "but living among them I've witnessed the kind of love, mercy and compassion that our scriptures describe."

"Wolves in sheep's clothing would be my guess," Steve said. "With riches gained through the misfortune of others. Have you seen their casino? It's the jewel of the Strip—shining bigger and brighter than all the rest. The kingpins of gamblers and thieves."

"Sounds like you've been inside," Damaris replied.

"Only to better understand the wiles of the enemy and better win the lost."

Damaris worked to not roll her eyes. Were these truly the beliefs that until now she'd wholeheartedly embraced? Steve sounded less like her dad and more like her grandfather.

"But that job's only temporary, right?" Lori asked.

"It's a six-month contract," Damaris replied.

"Six months and you get a vacation?"

"No."

"You said you're going overseas."

"Yes, but not on vacation. As part of my job. There are medical options not yet available here that might give Noah, and other victims of paralysis, the chance to walk again."

Philip leaned forward, as he listened intently. "You're planning to travel with an unmarried male?"

"I will be traveling with my patient, along with members of his family and other medical staff."

"Your father is okay with that?" Steve asked.

"I'm an adult," Damaris snapped. "My father doesn't control my work, or my life."

"Steve doesn't mean to upset you," Lori said, in a caring tone. "He, we, are all concerned about the short- and long-term effects of you working so closely with non-Laymen. Your father spoke at length with Philip. He's beside himself with the fear that you'll lose your way."

"Or find it," Damaris mumbled, chagrined but not surprised that she'd been a topic of conversation between Philip and her dad. She cleared her throat. "I appreciate your concern and will speak to my father. But I assure you, who I am and what I think are products of my own mind, developed through my own reasoning. I think Laymen could benefit by spending more time with the other—" she emphasized with air quotes "—people like the Breedloves, before being so quick to judge them."

The dinner conversation never fully recovered. Later, when Steve asked for her phone number, Damaris told him flat out that she wasn't interested. When Lori mentioned seeing her at church the next Sunday, she made no promises to attend. Driving back to Breedlove, Damaris realized that what her dad, the Sullivans and the Boltons had tried to do might have backfired. Instead of their talk pulling her closer to her Laymen roots, they'd highlighted how quickly and dramatically Damaris's views had changed. Instead of running from that truth, she decided to embrace it, explore it and see what happened. Which meant no longer ignoring her attraction to Noah.

Perhaps by giving in and allowing him those liberties her mother feared, his spell over her would be broken and they could both be free.

this was his first trip to Scandinavia. He was excited, not only for the possibility of walking but because it was Damaris's first time out of the country and, as he was quickly reminded by her gasp as she entered it, her first time on a private plane. The CANN jet had been pretty impressive before its nose-to-tip upgraded renovation last year. Now its interior rivaled the wealthiest of royalty and corporate execs.

"You like it?" he asked, while leading her past a set of seats and down the wide aisle to the open-space living room, where his chair could be both accommodated and locked in place.

"I never knew something like this existed. It looks and feels more like a home than a plane."

"Exactly what my mom and the designer were going for," Noah replied. "Later, after dinner, I'll give you the full tour."

Dinner service began just minutes after the plane leveled off and just before a magnificent sunset announced the end of the day. Damaris's joy was contagious, making Noah feel light, almost boyish as he experienced the life he took for granted through her virgin eyes. He delighted in watching her try new dishes, like the trio of mini-appetizers that began the meal—caviar on pita tips, truffle-laced mac-n-cheese poppers and oysters Rockefeller. A glass of vintage pinot further relaxed her. Conversation flowed as smooth and easily as the wine. He flirted and teased, delighted when instead of meeting a wall of resistance, she flirted back. When the entrée arrived and Damaris moaned with the first tender bite of medium rare chateaubriand, Noah imagined his manhood twitched, as he focused on the sultry experience generated by a voyeuristic journey deep inside her. By the time dessert arrived, a decadent slice of triple chocolate fudge cake, the two entered a new type of intimacy while sharing gooey bites of heaven from the same plate.

Damaris accepted Noah's invitation for the last bite of cake. "That's the best meal I've ever eaten in my entire life," she exclaimed, then fell back against the plush leather seat. "Now all I need is a comfy bed and a thick, soft blanket and I'd be off to dreamland in five seconds flat."

"I was just thinking the same thing," Noah said. He reached for the buckle securing the chair and unlocked it. "Come on."

Damaris looked at him through sleepy eyes. "Where are we going?"

"On that tour I promised."

She got up and followed him toward the front of the plane where the other passengers lounged. Travis and Noah's personal assistant sat at a table playing chess. Adam and Ryan were watching a movie.

Adam looked up and paused the video. "Hey, you two." The couples chatted briefly before Adam said, "Do you ladies mind if we talk business real quick?"

"Not at all." Ryan unbuckled her seat belt and stood. "I'd love the time to chat with Dee anyway."

Noah watched Ryan pull Damaris to a couch on the opposite side of the plane, then turned his attention to Adam. Meanwhile Damaris, who rarely imbibed, gratefully accepted a liqueur-laced cup of coffee from the flight attendant.

"Enjoying the flight?" Ryan asked Damaris, after they'd been served.

"It's beyond incredible," Damaris replied. "I have no words."

"I didn't, either, on my first private flight. Couldn't believe people really lived like this."

"I'm glad Adam was able to come over with Noah. He's been fairly fearless through a life-changing event that would have felled stronger men. But he keeps a lot inside him, too, including the vulnerability and uncertainty that he certainly feels."

"Mom and Dad are coming, too," Ryan said, referring to Nicholas and Victoria.

"They've been extremely supportive, which is invaluable to a patient's recovery."

"I've never seen a more tightly knit family," Ryan admitted. "Before Adam, I didn't know this type of closeness existed. Meeting him changed my life."

"How did you two meet?"

"Adam and my brother Dennis went to high school together. He introduced us."

"Was it love at first sight?"

"Ha! Hardly. On the surface, Adam and I were as different as night and day."

"Really? To see the two of you now, I never would have guessed that."

"It's hard for me to remember those days because now, I couldn't imagine my life without him."

Funny, but at this very moment, Damaris couldn't see her life without a certain Breedlove brother in it, either. She was about to ask Ryan more questions when she heard Noah laugh before turning to come toward them.

"Enough talk about health and healing," he joked. "It's time to finish our tour."

"Talk more later?" Damaris asked Ryan.

"Absolutely! Maybe you can go with me to see the home of Hans Christian Andersen. So far, Adam is less than enthused."

"Didn't he write 'The Ugly Duckling'?"

"That and other wonderful fairy tales."

"I heard about that story as a child and would love to go."

They started down the aisle.

"Be careful, Dee," Adam teased. "Noah might try to show you more than the plane."

Damaris blushed at the bold comment, while wondering if and how Noah's earlier flirting might play out. It was the first time he'd shown that kind of interest since Travis returned and the massages ended, causing her to think she'd waited too long, ready to act on an attraction that Noah no longer felt.

Noah took the lead as they passed the area where the two had eaten dinner and showed her how all of the sleek sofas doubled as beds.

"Wow, how many does this plane sleep?"

"Comfortably? Ten or so, but up to twenty or more if we have to and include floor space. This is an Airbus that in its original design could carry a hundred and sixty passengers, so the designers had a large layout to work with."

He pointed out a deluxe full bathroom with a shower, tub and sauna stall, touting platinum fixtures gleaming against marble in subtle shades of gray. The next section of the plane held a formal dining table with seating for twelve, one that could be lowered into the plane's belly, turning the room into a theater. He showed Damaris a dedicated bedroom, a second smaller room used as an office/workout area and the master panel that allowed passengers to control temperature, lighting, window shades and entertainment devices without leaving their seats. They continued down a short hallway to a closed door.

"Now," Noah said, looking back at her, "this next one is my favorite room on the plane."

Damaris followed Noah into a master suite that defied description. While easily half the size of the one in her guest home, it was many times more luxurious with every amenity and convenience one could imagine or ever need.

Noah quietly watched Damaris take a turn around the room. She peeked into a doorway. "Another bathroom?"

"One of three," he said with a nod. "There's another one at the front of the cabin."

"I could easily live here," she said, sitting to test out the bed. "This mattress feels as good as or better than the one back home."

Noah yawned as he rolled to the side of the bed. "Yes, and I'm getting ready to take full advantage of it."

"It has been a long day. Would you like me to get Travis to help you get settled?"

"No, Damaris, if you don't mind, I'd like your help with that."

Noah's voice held a tenderness that brought Damaris's nipples to instant attention. She looked down, thankful the reaction remained hidden behind a padded bra.

"How can I lift you?" she asked, using her tongue to moisten suddenly dry lips.

Noah nodded toward a closet. "The portable bod-riser fits on that hook."

She looked up and noticed the gleaming stainless steel fixtures. "Portable, huh?"

"Dr. Okoye had a prototype specifically made just for me."

She walked to the closet and pulled out the compact, collapsible device and wheeled it over to Noah. Focused on its novel design and ease of function while helping Noah undress, Damaris's professional mask barely slipped at seeing the strong chest she remembered and his tanned, sculpted legs. The bulge in his black boxers, however, could not be ignored.

"Do you feel that?" she asked, in a voice she hoped sounded dispassionate.

Noah looked down, then smiled. "No, but I wish you would."

Damaris grew warm, everywhere. Being ready and acting out a desire were two different things.

"The seat detaches," Noah said, focused on the lifter. "Through the stainless steel snap hook on the side. After sliding the leather beneath me you reattach it here. The harness works just like the one at home." He returned his gaze to her, eyes bright and intense. "Think you can handle it?"

He spoke of the lift, but her eyes slid to his crotch. "Sure."

Damaris pulled back the covers. Noah removed his shirt and T-shirt. She eased him into the lift and expertly transferred him into bed, adjusted the pillows and pulled his legs beneath the covers.

"Sit," Noah commanded, patting the space beside him. She did. "Touch me."

Damaris took a breath before turning her body more fully toward him. She grabbed the elastic top of his boxers with both hands and pulled. His erection sprang up like a just-released cobra, swaying slightly as though moved by her charm. She was the one enchanted. Turning off thought she let feelings take over, taking him in her hands with a gentle squeeze.

"Do you feel that?" He shook his head. She dropped her hands and then stroked him from base to tip. "Anything?"

"No," he replied while gently rubbing her back.

She repeated the move, her fingernail accidently flicking his perfectly mushroomed tip. His already engorged shaft further thickened in her grasp. She looked up expectantly, Noah's eyes on it, too. "Anything?"

He shook his head. "Damn." Noah's head fell back against the pillows.

He looked so defeated. Damaris's heart fell. "It's okay," she whispered, climbing into bed beside him, a move that was totally unplanned. She kissed him then— deeply, passionately—as her fingers splayed across his hard abs. Noah caressed her face before deft fingers eased over her top, and then beneath it. He lightly brushed them across her skin. Goose bumps followed in their wake. Her nipples tingled, longing for the same experience her back had just enjoyed. Her hand slid to his toned, muscled arms with a reassuring squeeze of silent consent to go beyond the bra to her breast, heart and soul.

Noah stopped, and with a finger raised her chin to see her eyes. "Take off your clothes. I want to feel you, however, wherever I can."

It was a reasonable request, one her hardened nipples straining against soft cotton gladly welcomed. She sat up, removed her top and bra, then shifted to lie upon him. Their bodies touched. Noah moaned, buried a hand in her hair and drove his tongue into her moist cavern.

"Pants, too," he whispered, once they came up for air. "Take off everything. I want to…satisfy you."

Caught up in the moment Damaris quickly obeyed, without one shred of shyness. She removed her slacks and underwear, felt the dew of excitement and wonder spring between her legs. Her inexperience caused a moment of worry. There was no need to fear. Noah was in control and an expert teacher. With his tongue and fingers, he played her body like an instrument and created a melody so beautiful it almost made her cry. He stroked and caressed her, plunged his deft finger into her core. She writhed against him to stoke the heat he created, wanting more of a sensation she'd not felt before. He encouraged her to give in, let go, enjoy the ride. She did, gasping at the force of her release, amazed at the revelation of what all had just happened, and how at that very second she fell completely in love.

Utterly spent, she reached for the sheet as she slid down and cushioned her head on his chest. Noah's heart beat strong and steady against her ear. She rubbed her hand across his stomach, and lower, brushed it against the now-flaccid member. She waited for guilt to creep up and consume her, but it didn't.

Noah eased tendrils of damp hair away from her face. "You okay?"

She nodded against his chest.

"Are you sure?" he continued. "How do you feel?"

"A little embarrassed. But other than that…amazing."

He chuckled then, a low, satisfied sound that warmed her insides.

"How do you feel?" she asked, looking up to see his expression.

"Happy that I helped you come out of your shell. You have a beautiful body."

"So do you. It's the first time I've lain beside a guy

Eighteen

Once Noah and the gang reached Denmark, everything
changed. His plans for one-on-one physical therapy with
Damaris were put on hold. Wanting to take advantage of
every moment of his time at the center in hopes of seeing definitive results, they were taken from the airport directly to Forskning and met by Drs. Filip Sondergaard and
Yonni Virtanen. The team was excited about having the
prototype they'd worked on for over five years tested out
in a human. He was x-rayed, given several physicals and
prepped for a procedure made fairly noninvasive using
specially designed implant needles and topical anesthesia.
A series of stimulator electrodes were inserted along his
spine's injured vertebrae, designed to work in conjunction with a formfitting pair of knee-length rubber shorts,
similar to scuba gear, threaded with electrical current to
activate the mini wonder discs.

Eight hours later, an exhausted bunch piled into a van and headed to the home they'd rented just outside town. While Noah had been in surgery, Damaris and his Nevada team had been given in-depth instructions and taken through the initial training of the program for his recovery. Noah was asleep before they'd driven out of Copenhagen's city limits. Between the rigorous schedule planned by the doctors and the ever-changing, fast-moving project back home, he was going to need all the rest he could get.

The next day, after an early-afternoon appointment with the doctors, a light workout with his bionic pants and absolutely no private time with Damaris, Noah settled into the home's airy office handling last-minute preparations for an upcoming videoconference. A constant flurry of emails and text messages had gone back and forth between team members. His brothers had rearranged their schedules to help implement the revised plans and keep the project on schedule. Clearly, everyone believed the Laymen problem had been solved and were moving quickly to implement the changes. Copenhagen was nine hours ahead of Las Vegas so just before six that evening, he sat in front of a large TV screen to head what would be a 9:00 a.m. meeting with the team back home.

A chef had been rented out with the house. She entered the home office, where Noah had set up shop. A breath of fresh air, otherwise known as Damaris, was just behind her.

"Hello, beautiful."

"I know you're busy," Damaris responded with a glance toward the chef, obviously uncomfortable with his public praise. "I saw her coming this way and decided to check in, make sure there is still no soreness or pain."

"There's a little pain," he said, eyes low, voice sexy

and filled with innuendo. He nodded toward the portable monitoring device she carried. "Nothing that can't be fixed."

He smiled at the telltale rosiness of unease that crept up from her neck. He loved pushing her buttons. No time for that, though. The chef, who'd picked up an empty dish from the silver serving tray and set down a fresh pitcher of lemon water and a clean glass, stood silently by.

"Alma, correct?" Noah asked.

"Yes," the middle-aged woman replied. "Excuse me. Can I get you anything else, sir? Some juice perhaps, or another cup of tea?"

"No, thank you," Noah responded. "The salmon was delicious."

"Thank you. Please, if you need anything just ring the buzzer above your desk."

Noah nodded, his eyes on Damaris as the chef quietly left the room. "Your turn."

"Oh, okay." Damaris set the device on the desk, ready to take his temperature.

"Not for that." He pulled Damaris onto his lap. "It's your turn to ask if there is anything you can do for me."

"Oh. Well, is there?"

A flicker on the screen caught Noah's eye. "Dang it, not now." He gave Damaris a quick peck on the lips before easing her off him. "I've got to handle this meeting, but definitely want time with you later."

He watched her retrieve the device and checked out her sexy exit before turning his attention back to the countdown clock on the screen. When the computer's appointment clock hit zero, the picture came on, revealing an executive conference room. Guys from the department waved and shouted out greetings.

"That's a great office, Noah," one of the junior execs noted. "But is IKEA the only store in that place?"

"Hey, it's good stuff," Noah replied, laughing off the comment.

Sidney Beck, VP of Expansion under Noah, held up an oversize coffee mug in greeting. "Don't let my wife hear you talk bad about it," he admonished the junior. "Half of our house is furnished with their products. I should buy stock in that store."

Personally, he appreciated the sharp, clean aesthetic of the Scandinavian designs. How they seamlessly blended functionality, minimalism and style. The casual chat continued as the chairs around the conference table filled. Once the select group of key players who'd been invited had arrived and taken their seats, Noah officially began the meeting.

"Good morning this evening," he began, then got right down to business. "I understand the Laymen have received word of our Manning Valley purchase?"

"Absolutely," Sidney responded, his startling gray eyes boring into the camera. "To say they are displeased would be an understatement."

"*Pissed* would be more accurate," Nick said. "*Shocked* and *befuddled* work, too. Moving the project out of their county and therefore out of their direct control is a move they hadn't expected."

Noah had learned how to navigate the real estate business from the best of them, his father. Using the art of the unexpected was one of his foundational rules.

"Any direct communication?"

"No, but my Layman insider said they called a special meeting to discuss what to do next, that they're thinking about trying to block this on the state level."

"How, with the Supreme Court?" Noah asked.

Sydney shrugged. "I'm sure they'll use whatever legal means are at their disposal."

Noah's brother Christian leaned back in his chair. "Don't worry, Noah. Our attorneys are already on top of it. They've retained a guy who's an expert on Utah, the Laymen and the history of gambling in that state. He was born and raised there and used to be part of the church. Our guys say he has a personal ax to grind."

"What's his name?"

"Thomas Riley."

Noah typed the name into his notes.

"And get this," Nick said, a gleam in his eye. "He grew up with one of the project's fiercest opponents."

"Who?"

"Franklin Glen."

Noah's brow rose. "You're kidding me."

"Seems confident he can get Glen to back off. Says he knows something about the elder's past that would tarnish his image, lessen his influence with the Laymen community."

Sydney cleared his throat. "Get him to fold, and the rest of their contingency will crumble."

Noah thoughtfully stroked his chin as he absorbed this news. What could be so detrimental to Glen that he'd end his objections? Given his growing feelings for Damaris, would he want to be the man to expose it?

"This isn't personal, it's business," Nick said, as though reading his mind.

Another team member nodded. "Remember, business negotiations are no place for being nice."

"I agree," Sidney said. "Whatever it takes to get this

project moving and calm down our investors. These delays and legal battles have cost enough as it is."

"Lydia, set up a phone call for me with Thomas Riley. If he's set to potentially assassinate someone's character, I want to know what type of bullets he's using."

The call lasted another hour, and left Noah drained. Being reminded of the ongoing opposition from Damaris's dad caused him to consider the possible consequences of a continued romance with Damaris. That she was inexperienced was something he didn't take lightly. If the procedure made it possible for him to have a sexual relationship with her, could he, if required, condone also taking down her dad?

For now, there was too much going on to worry about it. His physical condition hadn't improved. There was no time to spend with Damaris alone. When not at the prestigious research center just outside Copenhagen, he was back at the house handling what was now called Project MV, for Manning Valley, while being further analyzed by researchers, scientists and the medical team.

A week passed with no change in his condition. Noah tried to remain optimistic, had been told not to expect results overnight, if at all. He thought he'd prepared himself for the long haul. Now that the plans for the casino in Manning Valley were progressing, it was important for him to closely oversee everything that was happening. A responsibility handled much easier if he could walk!

He removed his shirt and buzzed for either Roy or Travis to help him remove the rubber shorts. Having seen no physical progress made an intense day longer. He rolled over to a window that looked out on a lake. A fresh snow sparkled under a bright, full moon. Stars dotted the inky blue sky. In spite of his will not to entertain them,

thoughts of doubt ticked the edge of his mind. Doubt that
what the doctors thought foolproof was truly innovative.
Doubt that he'd ever walk. He heard the click of the au-
tomated door and breathed a sigh of relief. He wanted to
get out of the constricted rubber and more, didn't need
to be alone right now.

"About time," he said, whirling around. The rest of
the comment died on his lips. "Dee."

"Hello, Noah."

She wore a loose, flowing maxi, the kind Ryan liked.
Her hair was down, and damp, as though just out of the
shower. She looked soft, sweet. Noah imagined tasting
every inch of her skin.

"Where's Travis?"

"I told him and Roy that I'd take care of you."

"Why?"

She reached him, then boldly sat on his lap. "Because
it almost feels as though I'm being avoided. Then I told
myself to stop being selfish and remember how much
you have on your mind."

She reached over, caressed his face. Her smile filled
the room, her eyes shone with desire. She kissed his
cheek, then slid her lips along his jaw to his ear.

"I know you don't believe in such foolishness," she
whispered, before outlining his ear with her tongue. "But
I've been praying for you. I have a good feeling about
you walking again."

Noah was set to object but just then she shifted,
her luscious backside pressed against his crotch. Even
through the rubber he imagined he felt it, and responded.
Damaris felt it, too. She eased off his lap, skimmed his
rubber-clad thighs with her fingernails. "I know they

serve a purpose, but do you want me to help take these off? You've been in them for hours."

She didn't wait for an answer. Just wheeled him over to the lift, slid the holster under his body, got a grip on the sides of the shorts and pulled. He was naked beneath them. She slid the pants to his ankles, then worked to remove them. When she straightened, it was to the sight of Noah's dick—hard, waving—like a welcome sign. A slight widening of the eyes was her only reaction, before maneuvering the holster over and lowering him into bed. She sat down next to his hip, causing Noah to wonder what happened to the bashful church girl and who was this take-charge vixen?

"Do you feel anything?" she asked, pointedly eyeing his penis.

"No."

She reached over and wrapped her fingers around it, rubbing up and down. "What about now?"

A shake of the head was all he could manage, watching incredulously as she lowered her head. There was no way. It couldn't be. She wasn't going to... "Ah!"

Forget about walking. The feel of her soft, wet lips on the tip of his dick made him feel like he could run out of the room! He gripped the chair with both hands, watched in shock and awe as she nibbled, licked and kissed it. Then he closed his eyes, leaned back his head and focused on the moment. It felt so good. She felt so... *Wait a minute.*

"Dee."

She looked up, smiled and continued to please him.

He reached out, put a firm hand on her shoulder.

"Damaris."

"Yes?" Her eyes filled with concern.

"It's… I feel something. I can feel you!"

Needless to say this new development changed the vibe. Damaris hurried from the room, raced back to cover his nakedness, then ran out again. She returned with Travis and Roy, Victoria not far behind. They called the doctors, who suggested he note any further changes throughout the night and come in first thing the next morning.

Filip and Yonni were there when he arrived.

"Good morning, Noah," Filip said. "Your phone call was quite something."

Yonni nodded, his excitement restrained. "Indeed. What happened? Tell us everything."

It took effort for Noah to not look at Damaris, the only one who would ever know all that occurred.

"I'd just gotten undressed when I felt…a sensation. That's when we called. Later, there was tingling and other sensations, a muscle twitch, or similar."

The doctors exchanged a look. "Let's get you into the lab."

A short time later, Noah was in a private hospital room surrounded by Victoria, Damaris, Travis, Cole and a team of specialists. X-rays were taken and tests were performed for nerve detection from waist to toe.

"There are definitely signs of improved feeling in parts of your lower extremities," Dr. Sondergaard concluded, as some of the special equipment used to work on him was wheeled out of the room. "I don't want to speculate prematurely, but what we'd hope might happen could in fact be occurring right now."

"The bruised area of my spinal cord is healing?" Noah asked cautiously, even as sparks of hope burst in his brain.

"We shouldn't get ahead of ourselves, but your improved ability to feel is indicative of nerves now responding that previously were not. You've also regained some flexibility in the lower area of your back. Minimal, but even so an upgrade from what I saw earlier this week. We'll have more information for you in an hour or so. Until then you have some family members that are probably pretty anxious for an update."

Noah left his private room at the research center feeling cautiously optimistic. His wishes and the pretty nurse's prayers may get answered after all.

Nineteen

Damaris looked up from her cell phone and gazed out of the window as the plane flew past the Breedlove estate and the landing strip came into view. A return to Nevada was a return to reality, when she'd have to unravel her feelings and deal with her father, who, given the voice mail messages she'd just heard, was upset that she'd left in the first place. Her feelings were jumbled, the line between professional and personal totally shattered. She took full responsibility. What happened wasn't Noah's fault. She just needed to know what this was that had developed between them. And she needed Noah to tell her. As if prompted, he materialized beside her.

"A lot different than in Denmark," he remarked with a nod to the view.

"Totally."

He locked his chair into position, then pulled out his phone. "You ready to be back in the real world?"

"Not really."

Noah stopped scrolling and looked up.

"I turned on my phone a little while ago. There were several messages from my family, my dad. He's upset that I flew to Denmark without telling him. I told my mom," she added.

"Any regrets?" he asked with an unwavering gaze.

Her eyes held as she gave her answer. "None."

The plane landed. Everyone was exhausted. The entire team was given the night and the next day off. Damaris shared a quiet ride in the van with Noah, but, after a brief hug, walked to her unit and pulled her luggage inside. She'd just filled the tub and was about to strip and enjoy her first bubble bath since moving there when her home phone rang.

"Hello," she mumbled.

"Damaris?"

"Yes."

"It's Walter, the guard at the front gate."

"Yes, Walter. How can I help?"

"Your dad wants to speak to you."

"My dad? Why did he call you when they have both my home and cell numbers? Wait, how did he get yours?"

"He's not on the phone, Damaris. He's at the gate and says he's not leaving until he sees you. Should I let him in?"

Shock added to Damaris's already sapped mind, rendered it totally blank. Hearing her father's raised voice in the background, and the guard's calm replies, gave her the jolt needed to move.

"I'm coming out," she blurted. "Tell my dad to give me five minutes. I'll be right there."

Damaris hurriedly pulled on a pair of jeans and the sweater she'd just thrown in the hamper. Her dad, here, in Vegas? And not just Vegas but the town of Breedlove, at the gate of the family's estate? She slipped into a pair of ankle boots, grabbed her coat and car keys and ran toward the garage. Seconds later she was speeding down the picturesque private lanes. Currently unable to formulate a complete sentence in her head, Damaris had no idea how she'd talk to her father.

She arrived at the gate. Her father stood pacing outside a rental car, his face a mask of worry and pain. In that moment, her thoughts shifted. Had something happened to someone in the family? Had they been trying to reach her for an emergency when she'd purposely been unavailable? She got out of her car and walked through the gate, shivering against the cold.

"Dad! Why… What are you doing here? Did something—"

"What am I doing, Damaris?" Franklin countered, a bit too calmly. "What are you doing? That's what I came here to find out and I'm not leaving until I get an answer."

The guard approached them, just as another member of security pulled up in his car.

"Is everything all right, Ms. Glen?" he asked her.

"I'm her father," Franklin stated, agitation raising his voice.

"Dad, please, this is private property that is heavily guarded with cameras as well as personnel. You can't just show up here."

"How else was I supposed to speak with you, Dee, when you don't return my or your mother's calls?"

"You both know I've been out of the country. We just got back, not even an hour ago. Mom knew I had no international plan and would communicate by email or Skype."

"Did you?"

"No," Damaris belatedly realized. "The schedule was so intense over there and combined with the time difference I just... I'm sorry."

The guard cleared his throat. Damaris hadn't realized he still stood close beside them. "Would you like to use the guardhouse, ma'am? It's warmer in there."

"Thanks, Walter. We'll talk at my home. Will you please open the gate?"

She returned to her car and braced for confrontation, too tired for anything but truth. She was no longer Daddy's little girl. She was a woman, a nurse, performing a legitimate job with an amazing family. She'd developed feelings for a man outside the faith. She felt bad doing so would disappoint her father but knew that what she felt for Noah was not wrong. Hopefully she'd put whatever concerns her dad had to rest, send him on his way and take the bubble bath she'd dreamed of.

She drove slowly, her dad following in his rental, seeing the grounds anew as through her father's eyes. Would he appreciate the jaw-dropping beauty of a landscape that fed her soul, or would he perceive the opulence as evil?

She pulled into the driveway, not the garage. Her father parked behind her. He got out, his eyes taking in everything around him, including her house, before finally falling on her with an expression she couldn't read.

"Who lives here?"

"I do, Dad. Let's talk inside."

"I want to know who all I'll be dealing with, and prefer not to interact with outsiders."

"It'll just be us. Come on." Damaris opened the door and led her dad into the living room.

"You live here alone?"

"Yes. There are guesthouses for some of the people who work here."

"Everyone gets their own home, not their own room?" He shook his head. "Such waste and extravagance when people are homeless."

"Not everyone."

Frank crossed his arms. "How did you qualify for such high living?"

"It's because I'm Noah's nurse, Dad. He lives next door."

"He what?"

"Dad, please, can we discuss this calmly? I'm sorry for not keeping in touch with Mom or returning your calls but it was a strenuous, exhausting trip. I don't want to argue."

"Don't you have regular hours?"

Damaris smiled. There was nothing regular about the Breedloves. "My job doesn't come with set hours, but I love it." She walked over to the couch. "Join me?"

He did, on the edge of the cushion, as though cooties covered the back.

"I feel that I'm making a positive difference. A bath followed by a good night's sleep and I'll be okay."

"You are not okay. You're changing and don't even know it. Look at you! Look at your hair."

Damaris had forgotten about Ryan flat-ironing it while they talked on the plane. "It was just to try something different. You don't like it?"

"You look worldly. Like them."

"You're right, Dad. I am changing."

"I knew it." He shook his head sadly. "I knew that once you left us, you'd lose your way."

"That's how it may appear to you." Damaris spoke softly, aware that their relationship would be forever altered after this. "To me, it feels like I'm finding it. Who I am and how I really feel about myself, the church and its beliefs. Not everyone outside the faith are the monsters I expected. The other people I work with here, for instance, are gracious, and compassionate, and kind. I've grown to respect the Breedloves, and admire their close-knit family. They're not evil people, Dad. They're—"

A sound interrupted her explanation, before Noah's voice came through the intercom.

"Dee, you okay?"

"I'm fine. Do you need me?"

His voice changed, lowered. "Of course."

"My dad's here." Said too forcefully, too quickly and too late, according to her dad's raised brow.

"Your father, Frank Glen? He's at your house right now?"

"Yeah. I forgot to keep in touch with Mom while overseas. He came to check on me."

"Hello, Mr. Glen. Noah Breedlove. We met, briefly, about a year ago. I head up a project for the CANN—"

"I know who you are."

"Excellent," Noah responded, not missing a beat. "I'd love to talk with you. How long are you here?"

"Just long enough to get my daughter packed up and back home."

A sustained pause, and then, "Dee, you sure you're all right?"

"She's fine."

"It's okay, Noah. I'll call you later."

"You may call him once we're back in Salt Lake. But you're leaving with me, tonight."

Damaris turned off the intercom. "Dad, this is my job. I have a patient. I can't just leave!"

"This isn't up for discussion, Damaris. I refuse to lose my child to this place." He stood, his look one of a made-up mind. "It's clear they have the resources to replace you ten times over. I'll pay to have your belongings shipped, or replaced."

"Dad." Damaris stood, too, the combination of exhaustion and strong emotion putting her near tears. "I'll come for a visit soon, I promise. But I can't leave now."

"Then you have no reason to come back at all. You can choose to live in disgrace here, with this family. Or you can come home to the people who love you, who truly have your best interest at heart. Weigh your decision carefully, daughter. Because you can't have both."

Twenty

Resisting the urge to barge through their shared door almost killed him. Of course, he couldn't. He had no right. Franklin was her father. It was her home. She could invite in whomever she wanted, even the bane of his existence for the past twelve months. To take his mind off the conversation happening next door, he picked up his phone to have one of his own.

"Yes, son."

"Hey, Dad. I'm not sure whether or not I thanked you for joining us in Denmark. I appreciated having you there."

"There's no need to thank me. It's what dads do. I'm so glad to have gotten there in time to meet all of the people working on that device, who put everything together to help you walk."

"I'm not there yet."

"You will be."

"That's the plan. Hey, Dad, I'm checking out the property in Manning Valley next week. You should join me."

"Chris told me the team had put in an offer. He said it's about forty acres of prime real estate."

"Backed up to the mountains and close to the freeway. Most important, it's out of the county where the Church of Laymen rule. We close in two weeks."

"I gotta hand it to you, Noah. You're doing the impossible. I'm proud of you, son."

"Thanks, Dad. We've cleared a major hurdle but are still far from a done deal. You know better than me what all can happen during these kinds of negotiations. Don't pop the cork yet."

The doorbell rang. Noah checked the security monitors. "Hold on, Dad. Dee's at the door."

He put the call on hold and tapped the intercom button.

"Hello."

"Noah, it's Damaris."

"I can see that." He watched her eyes scan the doorway and light on the lens. She wore no makeup and her hair was wet, probably just out of the shower. His body responded, despite her forlorn expression. He pushed a button. "Door's unlocked." Then, "Let me call you back, Dad."

"Is Dee okay?"

"That's what I'm about to find out."

He met Dee in the living room, looking small and vulnerable, totally unlike the ray of sun that normally shone whenever she was around. He remembered the woman who took care of him right after the accident. The cheery demeanor and confident assurance that all would be well.

That he would walk again. He was determined to make her situation better now, the way she did his back then.

She walked in and sat on a couch by the wall.

"What, no kiss or hug, nothing?"

Only then did he notice her too-bright eyes, and the tears that threatened.

"Baby, come here. What did your dad say? I'm worried about you."

She shook her head. "I'll just start crying again. I've done enough of that already."

"Talk to me, Dee. What's going on?"

"I have to go home."

"When?"

"Now." Damaris shared with him her father's ultimatum.

"I don't agree with him at all. But they're my family, Noah. When I ask myself if standing in my truth is worth it, if I can live never seeing or speaking to them again, the answer right now is no."

"Didn't you sign an agreement?"

"Yes, and not honoring it breaks my heart. I was totally blindsided, had no idea he'd come here. But I have no choice. Once I explain the circumstances, I believe Victoria will understand."

Noah could now imagine how Franklin felt when he learned they'd pulled the build out of Salt Lake City. He wanted to demand that Damaris stay and honor her contract. But this was already painful enough.

"I've spoken with Travis, who'll contact the rehab center. They have a roster of highly qualified on-call nurses. She'll have no trouble finding a replacement."

"What if I said I was happy with the nurse I have and didn't want to interview another one?"

Damaris stood and walked over to where he sat. She knelt down and placed her hands in his. "There are no words for how sorry I am, how I'm ashamed of my father's actions and am heartbroken that I won't be able to finish my contract. But I'm proud of you and so very happy that because of the new technology your walking again is just a matter of time."

"I appreciate that."

"I'll never forget the time I spent here in Breedlove. This beautiful land. Your family. My first time traveling out of the country. The only thing more beautiful than the Danish landscape and the city of Copenhagen is my experience of being there with you."

"The trip of a lifetime?" he said, his voice much lighter than his heart.

"Close," she said after a beat. "Hawaii would be the trip of a lifetime."

"You've never been there, either?"

"No, and that's my true dream vacation. Maybe someday." She rose up and hugged him. "I care for you deeply, Noah, and will miss you every day."

She stood and hurried to the door.

"Dee."

"Yes?" she answered without turning around.

"I agree that family should come first, but only when they put you first, too."

He watched her shoulders rise and fall, her hand still on the knob. The moment stretched on until he thought maybe she'd change her mind about leaving altogether. Finally, she opened the door and closed it softly behind her.

Noah swore the sky darkened and the room lost air.

The rest of the week he buried himself in Project MV

and learning to walk again. The rubber shorts were re-placed with a set of customized braces that also worked in conjunction with the implanted discs. The braces al-lowed him to stand upright, and then take his first step since falling down the mountain. He couldn't walk far, and only with assistance, but he was out of the chair. The word of his ongoing recovery spread fast within the com-pany and the town's inner circle. Women who'd not called him once since the fall now texted and left voice mails. But his conversation was reserved for the pretty nurse who'd always believed he'd walk again, and whose view of him stayed constant no matter his posture.

That Sunday, he pulled into the main estate's circular drive and parked the van. Instead of going to the front door, he wheeled himself down the drive and toward the chorus of voices drifting from the large patio out back. He rounded the corner and took in a beautiful tableau—a dozen of his favorite people, family by blood or by choice, enjoying beautiful weather, incredible food and each other.

He reached an empty space at the table, parked his chair and, with no greeting, reached for a pitcher filled with a drink he hoped contained alcohol.

"Still no word?" Victoria asked.

Noah shook his head, a slight smile appearing when Adam retrieved a decanter from the bar and poured more vodka into his Bloody Mary. "Thanks, bro."

"She feels terrible about what happened, son. I can't imagine the position she's in."

Nick turned to his twin. "I'm still waiting to hear ex-actly what happened."

"It's a long story," Noah said. "Christian, pass the menu."

He spent the next few minutes focused on brunch selections, not so much because he was hungry but to avoid the inevitable interrogation headed his way. Knowing he couldn't avoid them forever, he tapped a customized app on his phone and sent his order to their chef.

"We're not going to stop hounding you, bro," Nick said. "Mom wouldn't tell us—said it was your story. You might as well get it over with now, while we're all here. That way you won't have to repeat it."

Noah took a swallow of his drink, and grimaced as the strong liquor hit his throat then made its way to his stomach. He took another, smaller sip and set down the glass.

"Dee's father surprised her, flew down from Utah. He was here when we got back from Denmark."

"What'd he want?" Adam asked.

"In a word? Dee. Wanted to rescue her from the evils of gambling, including our family."

"How does he know about us?" Lauren asked.

Christian answered his wife. "He's a member of the Church of Laymen, the most vocal and powerful opponents to Noah's project in Utah."

"And you hired his daughter to work for you?" she asked Noah.

"That part wasn't planned." Neither was developing the strong feelings for her that he'd tried to ignore.

"He only found out later about their connection," Nick added. "And that Noah had met him in the project's early days."

"Yikes," Lauren said. "That's a sticky situation."

Christian rested a hand on his wife's chair, studying Noah. "This appears to be about more than an employee, no doubt an excellent nurse but one who can be replaced. Was there more going on? Did you develop feelings for her?"

Noah shrugged. "I don't know, man."

"He knows," Nick countered.

"You've never let anybody intimidate you or call the shots," Christian continued. "And if I remember correctly, you've got a business trip planned for next week. So what are you going to do?"

It took Noah a few days to come up with an answer. When he did, he booked a flight to Salt Lake City. It was time to confront his feelings, and Dee's dad.

Twenty-One

Dee sat across from Wendy at their favorite coffee shop, one week after leaving Nevada, nursing a cappuccino and a broken heart.

"I've ruined everything," Damaris quietly admitted. "Made so many mistakes. Coming back home instead of following my heart has been the worst of them."

"Come on, Dee," Wendy countered. "It can't be that bad."

Damaris fixed her with a stare. "It can't be worse."

Wendy reached across the table and squeezed Damaris's arm. "Tell me what all happened, friend. You were always so busy. We've barely talked. Start at the beginning."

Damaris launched into a recap of her time with Noah, from the time she arrived at the guesthouse until her dad showed up at the gate. Wendy listened intently. She asked questions for clarification but otherwise said little else.

"The problem was all the secrecy," Damaris surmised, after taking a break and finishing the coffee that had long grown cold. "I should have been truthful from the beginning—told Dad about the job offer and Mom about my feelings for Noah when they started to grow. Maybe I never should have taken the job. Had I never gone to Vegas, I wouldn't be sitting here hurting so much."

"You're in love with Noah," Wendy said. "That's why you're in so much pain."

Damaris shrugged. "I don't know. He's only my second serious relationship and it's been so confusing. I'm not sure I know what love is."

"I think you do know."

Wendy became quiet. Damaris looked up to see Wendy staring intently. "What?"

"I want to ask you something. Have you ever stopped to consider what Matthew has to do with everything that's happened?"

"Matt? He has nothing to do with it. He's dead."

"Exactly, and not only did losing him in that horrific accident tear you apart but that you'd continued to date him against your father's wishes filled you with guilt."

"I don't think—"

"Wait, Damaris. Please, hear me out. I know how much you love your family and can't imagine how the possibility of being cut off from them feels. But I wonder if you left Nevada and Noah because of that threat, or so as not to once again defy your father."

"Probably both." Damaris rubbed her arms against an inner chill. "I'm tired of talking about something that cannot be changed. What's up in Trauma? Think I can get hired back on?"

With that, Damaris effectively changed the subject.

She listened to Wendy's colorful recap of the hospital shenanigans, even laughed a time or two. But with her return home came the shroud of misery that had covered her world since leaving Breedlove. Wendy's statement returned, too. The one she'd denied at the coffee shop but that had played in her head nonstop since. Had all the barriers she'd created when it came to loving Noah come from the fear of losing her family, and especially again disappointing her dad?

Noah gazed out of a window with the peaks of Daredevil Mountain visible in the distance. He'd chosen the nearby restaurant on purpose, to discover how his body and mind would feel back at the place that changed his life. His muscles grew stronger every day and with technology's help, he was standing. One day, after regaining their full use and getting his ski legs, he'd go down the mountain again.

For now, though, he was content to sip the hot tea that had just been delivered and eye it from a distance. They'd made a bid on the land that shared the same mountain range. He'd met with Manning Valley's city leaders. There were two stops left on the agenda before boarding the plane, one for a conversation that was long overdue.

A punctual Thomas Riley walked up to the table. "Noah Breedlove?"

Noah stood to greet him. Thomas's jaw dropped.

"I thought you were…"

"I was. Still recovering." Noah held out his hand. "Nice to meet you."

They sat. "Would you like to order something? I don't have much time but…"

"You're a busy man. I won't take much."

Straightforward. To the point. Noah liked that. "I understand you grew up with Franklin Glen?"

Thomas nodded. "Knew his whole family. We lived on the same block."

"My understanding is that his family has always been Laymen."

"Back several generations."

"I can't imagine someone so deeply entrenched in the faith would do actions that went against it."

"Every religion has rules. Laymen among them. Some of the rules they deem righteous seem cruel to the average man."

What Noah learned in the next ten minutes changed his itinerary. He still planned to have a conversation with Damaris. But first he had to speak with her father. Acting purely on instinct, he called the church, made an appointment and directed his driver to the address the receptionist provided. Once there, Noah reached for the cane he'd been given to aid mobility and made a slow, determined walk to the executive office's entrance. Thankfully, the receptionist was just inside.

"Mr. Wright?" the kindly receptionist asked, after viewing her watch. "Mr. Glen is waiting for you. Please, go right in."

Noah approached the closed door and after a slight knock, opened it. Frank stood near a window with his back to the door. He turned around with a cordial smile that lessened slightly as he came forward with an outstretched hand.

"Mr. Wright?" he queried with narrowing eyes.

"No," Noah replied with a firm grasp of Frank's hand. "I'm Noah Breedlove."

Frank pulled back but Noah held the grip. "I apologize for deceiving your secretary, but it was imperative that I speak with you. For as much as we differ, we do share one common interest. Damaris."

Only then did Noah release Frank's hand and watch the elder man's head-to-toe perusal.

"My daughter claimed you were paralyzed."

"I sustained a crippling back trauma, yes, and, for a while, was immobile. Only recently have I been able to walk short distances, with the help of braces, this cane and technology still being tested. I am not yet healed, sir. In fact, it took considerable effort, almost all that I had, to walk through that door to face you like a man. It is painful standing here now." Noah nodded toward a chair. "May I sit down?"

He could see the wheels turning in Frank's mind, but correctly guessed he would be hard-pressed to deny a chair to an injured man who needed one. He motioned for Noah to have a seat, then took one behind a desk.

"What do you want?"

"Again, my apologies for making the appointment under an assumed name but I felt it was the only way you'd see me."

"As my daughter is no longer employed by you, how is this about her?"

I love her. That was the answer that immediately came to Noah's mind but since he'd not yet shared that with Damaris or processed it himself, the timing didn't appear right to let Frank know.

"Damaris is an exceptional nurse and was very happy

in Breedlove. By the time she left, our relationship had grown beyond that of patient/nurse."

"Then my timing couldn't have been better."

"If you'll forgive me, sir, your timing sucked."

Frank stood. "Nothing good can come from this conversation. I knew you'd be a bad influence on Damaris and I was right, just like I am about the moral decline a company like yours will bring to Utah. So if you're here to talk about either of those subjects you're wasting your time. You cannot date my daughter and that casino you think belongs here will never be built."

"Decisions arrived to based on your faith?"

"Absolutely."

"Yet you continue to visit your brother, even though that, too, is against the rules?"

Noah said this while staring at Frank and noted the look of utter shock before Frank regained control, schooled his features and came back around the desk.

"I don't know what you're talking about."

"I understand why it would be almost impossible to totally abandon Frederick, or Freddy as he's called. I know because, see, I have a twin, too. No matter what Nick ever did or didn't do, I could never turn my back on him."

Frank slowly sat down. When he spoke, his voice was low and raspy with emotion. "How did you find out about him?"

"That doesn't matter as much as knowing that with all of your loyalty to this institution, there is still a part of you that has a heart for someone who, according to the rules, should be put away and forgotten."

Franklin regained his stern composure. "What do you plan to do, try to blackmail me or Damaris with the knowledge of a crazy uncle she's never met?"

"I believe the politically correct term is *mentally ill* and no, I'm not here to blackmail you."

"Then why are you here, to try to get me to endorse the casino? To back down because you've changed locations? To get me to accept you and allow Damaris to return to Las Vegas? Neither will happen. You're wasting your time."

"I no longer need the church's endorsement to begin building. Regarding your daughter, I'm not here so that she can return to work. I'm here to tell you that my intentions are honorable. I care about Damaris. You've raised a beautiful woman."

Frank stood once again and spread his hands on his desk. "Let me tell you something, Breedlove. Your money might buy you everything else, but not my approval. You may have fooled her but I know your kind. You will never build a casino in Utah and you will never date my daughter."

He watched Frank walk over to the window, then joined him there. "As she is a grown woman, Mr. Glen, don't you think she should be the judge of that?"

"Obviously, her judgment is way off. Otherwise, she would have followed the rules."

An easy smile covered Noah's growing frustration. "You underestimate your daughter, sir. Dee strikes me as an excellent judge of character and a woman very much capable of making up her own mind. As for rules, there are exceptions, such as the one you make for your brother."

"That's different."

"How?"

"I don't have to answer your questions."

"Then I hope you'll answer mine, Dad," Damaris said,

as she quietly entered the room. "And once he and I are done talking," she continued, her eyes narrowed and now on Noah, "I'll have some questions for you, too."

Twenty-Two

The shock on her dad's face was no less than what Damaris had felt upon hearing Noah's voice coming from his office, what was being said and that he was standing unaided as he spoke.

"Iris wasn't at her desk and I heard voices…"

Frank looked from Damaris to Noah and back. "Is this your doing, Damaris, having him come here?"

"No, Dad."

"Not at all, sir—"

Frank whirled on Noah. "You. May. Leave."

The room became quiet. Nobody moved. The air fairly crackled around them. Finally, Noah turned toward Damaris. "Will you be okay?"

"I'll be fine."

He walked over to her. "Call me later?"

Damaris didn't respond.

"What about meeting me in an hour, at the Inn by Northwest? Please, Dee, we really need to talk."

After a curt nod from Damaris, he turned to Frank. "Mr. Glen, thanks for your time."

Had the daggers her father threw at Noah's back been real, she would have needed her nursing skills. Given what she'd overheard, however, she doubted even those would be enough to stitch up the wounds between them.

She crossed over to her father. "What happened?"

"That outsider manipulated Iris by lying to get an appointment. It was a waste of time."

"Was this about the casino?"

Frank snorted. "I think he's beginning to understand that that pipe dream will never happen. This negotiation was about you. But I shut it down."

"Dad…"

"We've had this conversation, Damaris. Your time with those people is over. I'm not changing my mind."

Damaris took a deep breath. "I've changed, Dad, and it has nothing to do with the Breedloves."

"I'm not going to talk about this anymore."

"Then will you talk about the man I heard Noah refer to as your brother?"

"No," Frank said. He sat and began rearranging papers on his desk, a clear sign of dismissal. "I'm not going to talk about that, either."

One look at the hard set of her father's jaw and Damaris knew he meant it. She left his office and dialed home on the way to her car. No answer. She tried her mother's cell phone. It went to voice mail, too. Who was this man Noah referred to as her dad's brother? Needing answers, Damaris started the car and drove over to where she could get them.

The Inn by Northwest, a chalet-inspired boutique hotel located on the outskirts of town, sat nestled against a set of towering mountains and next to a lake. Damaris had heard of it but never ventured inside, probably because a night's room rate was more than an average apartment's monthly rent. Once inside, the lobby took her breath away. Gold chandeliers against rich burgundies and dark woods gave the place an unexpected yet sophisticated old-world charm. After peeking into the quaint restaurant's dining area and seeing no familiar faces, she texted Noah, who replied with a room number. Her first thought was to demand that he come downstairs and meet her in public. The second one was that given what he might share about her father, privacy was needed. Either way, Damaris didn't plan to be there long. She crossed the lobby. Beside a small elevator tucked into the corner, a grand staircase led to the two upper floors. She walked down the richly carpeted hallway to the last door on the right. She knocked. Her heart raced.

Within seconds Noah stood before her, handsome as always, a steely resolve to his countenance, the merest hint of vulnerability in his deep, dark eyes.

"You're walking."

"Yes." He took a step toward her, then stopped, as though unsure if he'd get a caressing hug or a cursing out. "Would you like to join me for dinner or…"

"No."

He hesitated, but then erased the distance between them and pulled her into his embrace. Damaris cut the hug short. She was ecstatic about his improved health. But they needed to talk. What he did was not okay.

He grasped her hands. "How angry with me are you?"

"On a scale of one to ten, I'd say eleven." Damaris

pulled her hands back. "Why didn't you tell me you planned to meet my father? You had absolutely no right to do that, Noah, without letting me know."

"You might have asked me not to, and I wouldn't have wanted to go against that. But I was determined to speak with your dad."

"So you lied? Made the appointment in someone else's name? That after snooping around to dig up painful facts of his past?"

"I learned something rather interesting about Franklin, and yes, wanted to ask him about it."

"For what? To use against him in the push for your casino, to try to get the upper hand and possibly ruin his life in the process?"

"I have no desire to hurt your father, you or the church, but everything that's happened is what I felt I had to do."

"Which is?"

"To let him know how I feel about you, open the door for some type of dialogue, maybe reach an understanding. I care about you, Dee, and didn't want it to feel as though I was sneaking behind his back to date his daughter."

Damaris raised a brow. "You didn't want to sneak behind his back, but it was okay to sneak behind mine."

"As soon as that meeting was over, you were my next call."

"I should have been your first one."

"Perhaps you're right."

"But I wasn't. And what was that about my father having a brother?"

"Maybe you should ask him about that."

"I'm asking you!"

"If he wants it known, he should tell you."

"So not only did you lie but now you're keeping secrets, too?"

"Dee—"

"Did you or did you not lie to get in to see my dad?"

"He never would have seen me otherwise." Noah leaned against the wall and sighed. "Babe, I didn't come here to upset you and I'm sorry that you're angry. But I don't regret the actions taken to meet with your father. I did what I felt I had to do."

Damaris walked over and stood in front of Noah. "You know what? I believe you. I'm sure you thought everything you did was perfectly fine, the same way my dad justified showing up at my door unannounced and issuing the ultimatum that brought me back here."

Her voice fell to a near whisper. "I didn't like feeling manipulated then. And I don't like it now. It's understandable why you can't get along with my dad. You're too much alike."

She whirled around and headed for the door.

"Dee, wait!"

"What?"

"Don't leave angry."

"Leaving is the only chance my mood will get better."

Noah pushed away from the wall and came toward her. He tried to hide the effort it took to walk completely unaided. Damaris noticed. A twinge of guilt hit her heart. Like Noah, she hid her pain, too.

"I don't leave until tomorrow," he said, as his hand gently clasped her arm. "Stay with me?"

Damaris shook her head, then opened the door. "I'm thankful to see that you're walking, Noah. But I can't stay. Goodbye."

* * *

Damaris drove home in a daze. Once there, she went straight to her room. She was right to call Noah out on his manipulative actions. But why did she feel so bad?

A soft knock at the door disrupted her thoughts. "Honey?"

"Yes, Mom."

"Franklin told me about Noah. May I come in?"

Seeing Bethany almost brought on the tears that threatened. Damaris swallowed them and told herself to be strong. Face the truth. She and Noah were over.

"I don't want to talk about him," she informed Bethany, shortly after her mother had taken a seat on the bed. "I want to talk about my uncle, Freddy, and why I'm just now hearing his name."

Over the next half hour, Damaris learned about her father's twin, Frederick Allen, a troubled young man who'd been diagnosed with a mental illness shortly after turning eighteen. A fraternal pair who'd been pitted against each other and therefore never close, who were further distanced by a stigma Franklin tried hard to avoid. By the time they turned twenty-one, he'd become a youth leader in the Church of Laymen, who believed mental illness was brought on by lack of faith and disobedience. Those diagnosed as such were to be avoided at all costs.

"With the more visible position, Frank totally changed his social circle and cut off all contact with Freddy. When their parents died, he placed him in an assisted-living facility and the secret visits began.

"He loves the church and his brother," Bethany finished. "It's been one of his greatest burdens."

Damaris absorbed the news in shocked silence, realizing her dad had asked of her something that he himself could not do—cut someone she loved completely out of her life. It was a burden she wasn't sure she could bear.

The following week, needing space away from family and time to think, Damaris moved out of her childhood bedroom and in with Wendy. She went back to Manning Valley Medical—working, and miserable. Though still upset about the stunt pulled on her father, she missed Noah more than a fish missed water and hadn't accepted his calls. Hearing his voice broke her heart. Not being able to see him was even more painful. But her father had made his position clear. If she went back to Noah, he would disown her.

"Hey there."

Damaris looked up from a tray of uneaten food. "Hey, Wendy."

"Are you losing weight?"

"Probably. Not much appetite."

"Why don't you go back already?"

"Because I don't like being lied to or feeling manipulated."

"Noah tried to talk, but you wouldn't listen."

"I'm a grown woman. He should have come to me first."

"Maybe he didn't for the same reason," Wendy quietly responded. "Because he's a grown-ass man.

"Call him, Dee. Hear him out. Life won't be the same without knowing the whole story."

"How will it be without my family?"

"If they really love you, they'll come around."

March snows gave way to April showers. Though still distant with her father, Damaris and her mom talked almost every day. Bethany worried about Damaris and agreed with Wendy that if her daughter truly had feelings for Noah, avoidance was unhealthy. The two needed to talk. Damaris knew she had to go one step further. She needed to see Noah. It was time to return to Las Vegas.

"Good morning, babe," Noah answered the next day.

"Good morning."

"I'm headed to a meeting and only have a couple minutes. What's up?"

"We need to talk."

"About?"

Damaris heard the pain beneath the anger in his voice. "I shouldn't have left so abruptly when you came to Utah. Yes, I was angry about your visit with my father. But you deserved the chance to tell your side."

"And you deserved to not have been blindsided by my visit. I'm sorry about what happened, babe. Looking back, I could have and should have handled that situation differently. Not including you in something involving your family, not telling you about my plans or your uncle was wrong. You should have been the first person to know everything. Believe me, if given the chance, something like that would never happen again."

Noah finished his meeting, then called Damaris. They talked for three hours that night and every day afterward. Both were delighted that Noah's mobility continued to improve. By the time the end of the month rolled around, Damaris stopped fighting the inevitable and booked a flight to Las Vegas. She hoped Wendy was right and her family's love would prevail because Damaris wasn't returning for a simple visit. She was moving back to Breedlove...to live.

Twenty-Three

Over the summer, Noah was busier than ever. The bill for virtual card-cash gambling in Manning Valley finally passed, a first for the state. On top of the continued travel back and forth to Utah were monthly trips to Denmark for the as yet non-USA-approved electrode treatments. He'd developed another passion: revolutionizing an industry to help those with spinal injuries. He and his twin, Nick, had formed a company, Breedlove Bionics, and become investors in the robotics company that helped him walk again. Then there was Damaris and their budding relationship. She was back in Vegas, adjusting to a new job, schedule, life. Fall arrived, then winter, with her still estranged from her family, still battling mixed feelings about leaving Utah. Noah encouraged her to take as long as needed to be comfortable with her choices. He was a patient man, supporting her no matter how long it took.

One Breedlove constant was the family brunch, where he was set to meet Damaris before spending a day enjoying her favorite new pastime, riding horses. As he turned the corner onto the estate's outdoor living space, he spotted Nick and Damaris with their heads together standing by one of the bars. She burst out in laughter, then noticed him approaching and tried for a straight face.

He offered a brief hug and kiss before asking, "What is he telling you now?"

"Blackmail material," Nick answered. "In case you get out of line."

Noah and Nick shared a shoulder-bump hug. "That's your job."

"You seriously tried to build a spaceship in seventh grade?" Damaris asked.

"I'm still trying to build one," was Noah's quick response. "If I get cleared for space travel, will you go with me?"

"Um...let me think about it...no." Said quickly, all of the words running together, which suggested her answer took no thinking at all. "The search for E.T. is all yours."

The rest of the family arrived. More than the delicious food and extravagant atmosphere, the Breedloves enjoyed each other. They all marveled at Noah's continued improvement and medicine's technological advances, which dominated early conversation.

"How many treatments are left, bro?" Adam asked, before biting into a double-decker sandwich.

"If my body continues responding the way it has, they might be over by the end of the year."

"After that you'll be totally healed?" Lauren asked. Of all the wives, she was the least informed on Noah's journey.

"I'll be able to walk without the aid of robotics," Noah said. "Whether or not one ever completely recovers from a back injury is hotly debated. That I'm walking at all is a miracle, and that there doesn't seem to be any lasting restrictions of my lower extremities is more than the doctors could have dreamed. If a little pain here or there is the price to pay for that freedom, I'll take it."

Nick sat back down after a second trip to the buffet. "My question is when do you think you'll be able to ski again?"

"That's not happening," Victoria chided.

"He should go as soon as possible," Nicholas countered, one of the rare times he and his wife weren't in total agreement. "The best way to get over the fear of a fall is to fall again."

The topics jumped from medicine to sports before centering on business and Project MV.

"I can't believe how quickly the bill passed once the location moved." Nicholas looked at Noah. "Why didn't that idea occur to you sooner?"

"All of the research done led us to Salt Lake City. It seemed the soundest economical choice. Insiders who thought they could sway church members fell through. We'd already bought the land, applied for permits, hired subcontractors. I had tunnel vision," he admitted. "Focused on a battle instead of the war."

"It takes strength to admit that," Victoria said. "You should also acknowledge the real reason you moved the operation to Manning Valley, why the bill was passed and you're set to begin construction." Everyone waited for the answer.

"Dee, of course! She's the one who pushed you to

think outside the box and when you did the results were brilliant."

Noah reached for his glass. "You're absolutely right, Mom. To you, Dee."

The table joined him. "Hear, hear!"

About an hour after brunch ended, Noah, Damaris, Adam and Ryan saddled up and took a leisurely ride. Conversation was good but minimal, with everyone content to enjoy the beautiful surroundings and the unseasonably cool day. Noah noticed Damaris being especially subdued. Later that night, after they'd returned to his home and were enjoying mugs of hot chocolate by the patio's firepit, he asked her about it.

"Come here, babe." They were sitting across from each other. Noah invited Damaris to sit on his lap. "What's going on?"

Damaris looked at him. "What do you mean?"

"Don't do that. I'm becoming fluent in Damaris. You were extra quiet during the ride. Why?"

She sighed, leaned her head against his shoulder and looked at the changing sky, a dusky blanket of turquoise turning to indigo, revealing thousands of stars. "It's my favorite time of year."

"And that makes you sad?"

"It might be the first one without my family."

"Do you think your dad would seriously forbid your family from coming to visit, and they'd listen?"

"Dad is going through a lot right now. I'm not sure what he'd do. You're lucky, Noah. I watched your father, and can see how much he loves you, how proud he is of all his kids. My dad still refuses to speak to me. Mom said he feels I've befriended his enemies and blames me for the bill going through."

"You know that's not true, right?"

"With my head, yes, but not with my heart."

Noah would have bet money that Damaris was wrong, that no way would her dad allow the holidays to pass without her. But when Thanksgiving rolled around, that was exactly what happened. She talked and video chatted with Bethany and a couple her siblings but Franklin made it clear that Damaris wasn't welcome back home and Bethany couldn't visit Las Vegas. The day was filled with turkey and the usual trimmings but for Damaris, little joy. Later, when the tears came, Damaris allowed them. Noah held her, and wiped them away. Each felt like acid and fueled his resolve. This would be the last holiday Damaris spent without family. He'd do whatever it took.

Twenty-Four

"Hawaii, darling? That's terrific!"

Damaris had just finished packing her bags for the week she and Noah were going to spend in the Aloha State over Christmas vacation. They'd be returning on the thirtieth, in time for the Breedloves' annual New Year's Eve bash. She knew that Noah had planned the trip to lift her spirits and that she should be super excited. But the truth of the matter was that in addition to Christmas, she'd just had a birthday. None of her family had been there. She missed them, and no amount of sea and rainbows could replace her mom and dad.

"Aren't you excited?" Bethany asked. "You've always wanted to go there."

"Yes, but I always imagined it would be with my family."

Bethany quietly replied, "Maybe someday."

Time to change the subject. "It's almost cookie season. Have you guys begun making the dough?"

"All we're preparing for is the birth of your niece. Your sister has four weeks to go and is as big as a house. Everyone believes the child will come early."

"I can't imagine not being there to help out. Baking cookies for the local shelters, military and single dads has been a tradition since before I was born. I wish Dad…"

"Me, too, Damaris. Know that I'm slowly, continuously trying to change his mind. It was easier for me. I don't agree with your current lifestyle, but I do believe your heart is in the right place. I also like what I hear about your young man, Noah. It took courage for him to face Franklin and admit how much he cares for you. These kinds of changes take time, but they can happen. Trust in that, okay?"

"Will you take lots of pictures for me, and maybe sneak a video call in sometime during the day?"

"I'll do what I can, sweetheart, but you're the one who needs to take pictures so I can visit that beautiful place through your eyes."

The doorbell rang.

"That's probably Noah, Mom. I need to go. Our plane leaves in about an hour."

"All right, sweetie. I love you."

"Love you, too."

Damaris went to the door and opened it. Instead of Ryan it was Elvis, one of the family's drivers.

"Noah asked that I come for you," Elvis explained. "He's tied up handling some last-minute business before your vacation begins."

A feeling of loneliness threatened. Damaris pushed it away. She was being selfish and ungrateful, focused on what wasn't happening instead of the blessing that was right in her face. Her wonderful, thoughtful boyfriend had planned a trip to Hawaii because he knew it was her favorite place and wanted to make her happy. There were worse ways to spend Christmas than having a dream come true.

Noah couldn't remember ever being ruffled. He was the brother with ice in his veins. But right now, while overseeing this latest project, neither *cool, calm* nor *collected* could be used to describe him. He could feel every nerve in his body and they all were abuzz.

He glanced over at Damaris, still sleeping beside him in the master suite of his brother Christian's private plane. Poor baby. He'd kept her up for most of the night and should have felt guilty. He didn't. The lovemaking had been too good. When she shifted and exposed a soft, toned thigh, he figured another round would be the perfect distraction.

He eased back the covers, slid his body down and kissed the tempting limb. He looked up. Nothing. He kissed it again, ran his tongue up to her hip. She frowned, turned away and partially exposed a silk-panty-clad cheek. Perfect. He ran his lips over her lusciousness, before lifting gently shifting her legs and settling his face between them.

Damaris gasped. "What are you doing?"

Noah's grin was mischievous. "Remember when you used your lips to help me feel? I'm returning the favor."

Noah ran his tongue between her folds—quickly, expertly—she could barely respond. He suckled and nibbled until her pearl became moist and words failed her completely, until her thighs shivered with the first orgasmic wave. Hard, thick and ready, he lifted himself and slid inside her, filled her completely and set up a slow, throbbing pace.

"Baby," she moaned, running her hands over his hard butt before lifting her hips and swirling them against him, in time to his beat.

"That's it, sweetheart," he encouraged. "Let your mind go, let your body be free. Let's make beautiful music together."

A couple hours and a powerful orgasm later, Noah felt infinitely more relaxed. He left Damaris in the shower, dressed quickly and reached for his phone to text Victoria.

We're almost there. All set?

No!

Victoria's response was immediate and not at all what he'd expected. The nerves returned full force. His mother was the queen of last-minute parties, could pull off one for a crowd of hundreds in less than a day. What was going on?

His phone lit up again. Last-minute changes to guest list.

Noah's heart dropped. Damaris's family? Were they not able to come?

Sorry, honey. Delay an hour, at least. Will text when coast is clear. Don't worry. It'll be fine.

Damaris finished dressing. They'd be landing soon and took seats up front. Noah placed an arm around her as he looked out the window. He could imagine her thoughts around this holiday season. Family. And her not with them. A part of him knew he was doing the right thing, no matter who did or didn't show up. The other part wasn't sure. Franklin seemed unmovable, willing to lose his daughter for the sake of the church. The celebration he'd planned for her had cost him a fortune. He knew she'd be pleased. Yet all of the money in the world couldn't buy the one thing Damaris wanted the most—unconditional love from her dad.

Noah couldn't imagine being estranged from his father. Was it right for Damaris to lose a relationship with hers because of him?

No way. The decision made, and his heart breaking, he tapped his mother's smiling face icon once again.

This whole thing is a bad idea, Mom. Tell everyone that something came up. Put them on planes tomorrow. I'll arrange for Dee and I to stay at one of our Maui houses, and show her the island once everyone's gone.

Victoria's response came screaming across satellites. ABSOLUTELY. NOT.

I can't come between Dee and her family, Mom.

The pause was longer this time, but she finally answered. You already did, son, the moment she fell in love with you. Don't give in to doubt. Follow your heart. It will always take you home. xoxo.

Not so easy, Noah wryly thought. Said heart was already in his stomach. By the time they landed it would be on the floor, on his feet or just beyond them. When

Damaris turned to face him, he pulled himself together enough to present a real smile.

"Excited?" She nodded. "Good. We're about twenty minutes from touching down."

"It's beautiful."

"It is."

"And very green."

"Yes."

"We'll be staying at one of your family's properties, right?"

"A CANN property, yes, with all of the amenities of one but not a hotel. It's a series of houses located on a private island, for the vacationer who wants to get away from it all."

"Like cooks and housekeepers and a concierge?" Noah nodded. Damaris sat up, obviously intrigued. "How does that work?"

"We have a network of employees that work to ensure the comfort of every guest. There is a chef for every home along with housekeeping, laundry, gardening and other staff. There are no cars allowed on the island but there are ATVs and UTVs, scooters and carts, a boat for quick access to the main islands and a variety of vehicles for water sports."

"It sounds incredibly expensive."

"It is. Fortunately there are people in the world with tons of money and nothing to do but find ways to spend it."

"I can't imagine it," Damaris said.

Noah smiled. *Soon you won't have to.*

The pilot announced the plane's descent into Honolulu. Noah and Dee fastened their seat belts to land. Moments later they walked off the aircraft, Damaris's eyes bright as she walked down the stairs.

"I've always considered Utah one of the most beautiful states in the Union," she said. "But those mountains are incredible. The clouds are so close I can almost touch them."

Instead of responding, Noah reached for her hand, content to listen to the ramblings of an excited first-timer taking in paradise. He also used her preoccupation with the new surroundings to exchange a few discreet texts with his mother and Nick. He also texted Bethany, hoping she'd found the strength to defy Franklin and attend her daughter's party after all.

Damaris's banter continued as they entered the airport. She squealed when presented with an exquisitely designed lei, and breathed in the fragrant smell of orchids.

"Thank you," she said as the young lady smiled.

"Aloha."

The next flight was on a smaller aircraft and took just over half an hour. They neared the exit. Damaris stopped. "Wait, where's our luggage?"

"Someone is handling that for us. Your clothing will be at the house when we arrive."

"Ah, part of the private home amenities." Noah nodded. "I could get used to this."

Instead of the usual town car, a tricked-out Jeep sat idling at the curb, with tinted windows, a fire-red leather interior and rims so gleaming Damaris could have used their reflection to put on her makeup.

"This is cool!"

"You like?"

"I love."

"I can see you tooling around Breedlove in one just like it."

A middle-aged man with curly black hair and gleaming brown eyes approached them. "Good afternoon, sir. Dale Tana."

"It's just Noah, man. Nice meeting you, Dale. Thanks for the wonderful weather."

The driver smiled, revealing bright white teeth against his weathered, tanned skin. "All my doing, Noah. You're welcome."

The easy banter continued as the Jeep sped along the road, Dale barely slowing along hairpin curves. Soon hard-packed dirt was traded for a well-paved road, seemingly carved inside a dense jungle of flowers and trees. They rounded a curve. Noah heard Damaris's sharp intake of breath. She'd seen it, the wide expanse of crystal-blue water behind La Damaris, the mansion bearing her name.

"Is that the ocean?"

Noah nodded. "The one we just spent almost six hours over, the majestic Pacific." He watched a myriad of happy feelings play across her face. To know he'd helped to put them there made him feel like a superhero. Life only got better when they arrived at the gate with *La Damaris*, a wrought-iron work of art, written in cursive, starkly contrasted with the bright white posts that held it.

"Noah, look! My name!"

"Well, what do you know."

"I never, ever see my name. But it's there, on the fence. How'd that happen?"

His eyes twinkled. "No idea."

"Wait… You?" Noah watched Damaris's gaze become misty as reality dawned. "You had them carve my name on the gate?"

"You like it?"

"I think it's the coolest thing that's ever happened to me. But why?"

He kissed her. Twice. "You ask too many questions. Let me show you the house."

A welcoming veranda surrounded the three-story wonder. Dale let them out at the front entrance, then continued on around back where the sound of another engine reached them.

"Part of the staff?" Damaris asked.

Noah shrugged. "I guess."

"It's just you and me, and only for a few days. How many people could that possibly take?"

Instead of answering, Noah opened the door and stood back to let Damaris enter first. Scents from a five-foot floral arrangement in the vast foyer wrapped around the couple like a welcoming hug. Deep bluish-gray paneling gave relief to the stark white silk-covered walls that flowed seamlessly into a great room that was more like magnificent. The furniture was high-end yet inviting— white leather couches, chairs upholstered in raw silk, mixed with accents of deep blue, onyx and sage. Modern art blended perfectly with restored antiques. Large paneless windows let in an abundance of light, the greenery of the meticulously landscaped yard and an unobstructed water view.

"This is so pretty," Damaris said, her voice a whisper. "Don't pinch me if I'm dreaming. I don't want to wake up."

Sounds of muffled laughter floated from the rooms beyond them. Damaris eyed Noah, her look slightly chagrined. "How many people have been hired to help us this weekend?"

"I'm not sure," Noah said. "But it sounds like more than I've paid for. Let's go have a look."

They passed through a library, then walked across an expansive dining room with a movable wall of pure glass. Noah slid the glass open. The sound of noises increased. They walked out on the patio, turned the corner and heard a chorus of voices.

"Surprise!"

The look on Damaris's face was easily worth the money the party cost him. That the Breedloves were there could be explained. They owned the property. But when she saw Wendy, and a few friends from Utah, tears formed in her eyes. The crowd parted. A beaming Bethany held out her arms.

"Mom?" Damaris made like a missile and flew into her arms. "What are you doing here?"

Bethany smiled at her daughter while wiping tears. "Your sister couldn't travel all this way by herself."

Damaris whipped around. "Stephanie's here?"

Stephanie laughed, coming out from behind a pillar. "Last time I checked." The sisters hugged. "This place is crazy," she whispered, "and has your name on the gate and everything. That's pretty cool."

"There's one more surprise," Bethany said. Damaris's eyes widened with hope. "No, not him," Bethany said. "Your brother, Charles, came, honey. He's changing out of wet swim trunks and will be down soon. Happy birthday, sweetheart."

Everyone who heard her echoed, "Happy birthday!" With that, the party was on.

* * *

Much later, around midnight, feet bare, hair gently moving with the breeze, Damaris stood on the balcony facing the water, and gave gratitude for her life. A sound startled her, before familiar arms wrapped around her from behind. She luxuriated in his embrace.

"Hey, handsome." She turned around. "I want to tell you something."

"What?" Noah kissed her cheek, her forehead, her lips and neck.

"You're pretty amazing, you know that?"

"I try." His hands slid up her arms. One finger flicked at the outline of a nipple, now clearly visible beneath the short silk robe she wore.

"How'd you do it?"

"Your family?"

"How did you contact them? What did you say to get Mom here without my father? There's no way he approved of their trip."

"I have a feeling your mom is stronger than you think, but it wasn't me who reached out. Mom contacted Bethany."

"Victoria. Of course."

"She knew I wanted this day to be special. That couldn't happen without some of your family here."

"It was great seeing Cole, too."

"He's been busy with a new job on the East Coast. But he wanted to be here, for both of us."

"I can't think of a way big enough for me to thank her, or you."

Noah wriggled his thick, black eyebrows. "I can think of a way." He kissed her. "Maybe two."

Damaris tried her sexiest moves as she took his hand and led them to the bed. For the next several minutes she let her lips do the talking. So did Noah. Their tongues, too. They nibbled and swirled and sampled each other, growing hotter by the second, each moan louder than the last.

"Baby." Noah placed a hand on Damaris's chest, and pushed her back gently. "Wait."

"I don't want to wait. I want to feel you inside me."

"I want that, too. But I need to do something first."

"What?"

He rolled over and opened a drawer on the nightstand. "I planned to do this at dinner tomorrow, but the time feels right now."

Damaris looked down. Noah held a small box covered with crystals. "An early Christmas present?"

"Your belated birthday gift. Open it."

With eyes still on him, she lifted the lid. Inside, the box was lined with crushed black velvet surrounding a perfectly round four-carat blue diamond solitaire. Her hand slowly rose to her mouth.

"Noah, it's stunning. I've never seen anything more beautiful in my life."

"It will look even more beautiful on you." He pulled the ring from the box, lifted her left hand.

Her jaw dropped.

His eyes sparkled. In that moment Damaris knew a handsomer man did not exist in the world.

"Will you do it?"

"Wear that big rock? Absolutely."

The twinkle in Damaris's eyes proved she'd understood the question.

Noah became serious. "Damaris Glen, will you marry me?"

"Yes, Noah Breedlove. Of course, I will."

Noah pulled the sash from her robe to reveal her naked body. "Damn, you're beautiful. I love you, baby."

She reached for his belt buckle. "I love you, too."

"Baby, hold on. I can't think straight." He pulled the silk fabric together to cover her body, reached for her finger and took a deep breath. "This might seem crazy, even ill-planned. I've always gone with my gut. Now my heart's in it, too. Tumbling down that mountain, waking up unable to move, I would never have believed anything good could come from that. But something phenomenal did. The rest of my life started there. I'm so happy that you'll share the rest of it with me."

He slid the robe off her shoulders, ran his hands over her breasts, across her stomach, down her thighs. He slid a finger along the seam of her heat. Desire burned in his eyes.

"You want to practice a little physical therapy, see if I can feel anything?"

Damaris again reached for the buckle on his pants and undid it. She unzipped them, slid a hand inside his boxers and stroked his dick.

"I want to see if I feel anything."

"Oh, baby. You're so sexy. I'll make sure you feel all of this…as often as you'd like."

Damaris hissed as Noah guided them down and slid a finger inside her, his tongue swirling to the rhythm of that same lazy beat. He took her over the edge, and while she shivered, slowly, gently, eased into her wet and ready paradise. She cried out, before relaxing so that he could go further. With their bodies, minds and souls fully connected, the first phase of his Sin City seduction was over. Another more poignant, deeper healing had only just begun.

* * * * *